THE PRIMROSE CONVENTION

THE PRIMROSE
CONVENTION

Jo Bannister

Chivers Press • Thorndike Press
Bath, England   Thorndike, Maine USA

This Large Pr 38212002833678 l, and by
Thorndike Pro Main Adult Large Print
Bannister, Jo
Published in 1 The primrose convention
Publishers Ltc [text (large print)]

Published in 1   DEC Q R   Press,
Inc.

U.K. Hardcover ISBN 0-7540-3253-1 (Chivers Large Print)
U.K. Softcover   ISBN 0-7540-3254-X (Camden Large Print)
U.S. Softcover   ISBN 0-7862-1383-3 (General Series Edition)

The text of this Large Print edition is unabridged.
Other aspects of the book may vary from the original edition.

Set in 16 pt. New Times Roman.

Printed in Great Britain on acid-free paper.

British Library Cataloguing in Publication Data available

Library of Congress Cataloging-in-Publication Data

Bannister, Jo.
     The primrose convention / Jo Bannister.
     p. (large print) cm.
     ISBN 0-7862-1383-3 (lg. print : sc : alk. paper)
     1. Large type books.   1. Title.
   [PR6052.A497P75   1998]
   823'.914—dc21   97-52115

PROLOGUE

Rain hammered the glass like an angry man demanding entry. At the desk beneath the window Philip Morris started violently enough to stick the stamp askew on the postcard he was writing. An orderly man, he tried to peel it off and start again; but Her Majesty was already resolutely attached to the back of a bad photograph of Edinburgh Castle and picking at her with his thumbnail only defaced the trailing edge of her diadem. He sighed, smoothed her over with his fist and dropped the card on to the open pages of the book beside him. It was not a new book. It was a much used and much travelled book. It had just returned from a fortnight under canvas in the Hebrides, and if he hadn't remembered to take it out of his pack it would have found itself on a train to Birmingham.

The window rattled again, an ill-fitting casement in a tall house tucked away behind St Giles's Cathedral where he'd seen a Rooms To Let sign when he first came to Edinburgh four years earlier. It had been his home base ever since, though he'd spent longer away than actually living there. But Mrs Mackey was an obliging landlady who watered his plants while he was abroad and, on receipt of a postcard heralding his return, would dust his room and air his bed. Once he'd come back unexpectedly to find the decorators at work: she'd put him in with her son until they finished, which was only a problem when the boy wanted to study maths while the engineer wanted to listen to 'Guns 'n' Roses'. After four years they were like family: Mrs Mackey was as glad to see him back from one of his jaunts as he was glad to be home.

But Philip Morris was no more designed for inertia than one of his machines, and sooner or later—typically after three or four months— someone in the Canongate offices of Webster Bryant (Civil Engineers) would mention in his hearing that they were looking for mission specialists to work on a bridge in Sarawak, a road in Colombia or a dam in a particularly inaccessible part of Wales, and he'd have blown the dust off his hard hat and checked his inoculations before anyone else could raise a hand. Even after four years it hadn't struck him that nobody else intended to.

The point was, Philip most enjoyed those parts of the job that his colleagues found most difficult. He had no family responsibilities, no obligations, not even a house to shut up. He could be packed and on his way in a few hours if necessary. And he enjoyed doing it. He enjoyed heading off somewhere he'd never been before, to take over a project someone else had already had enough of, with all the unfathomable problems that attend major construction works in distant lands.

Which was one reason he needed only a part-time home. The other was that, when he wasn't up to his ears in mud and D7s, his idea of relaxation was erecting a one-man tent on some blasted heath or spit of shingle, pulling up the collar of his anorak to meet the ribbing of his bobble hat, and watching birds. Philip Morris was a serious ornithologist who undertook scientific field surveys, sometimes for natural history organizations, often for his own research. Whenever he returned from somewhere hot and remote where corruption was the continuance of business by other means, he rewarded himself with a few weeks somewhere cold and remote where the thorniest problem was distinguishing a large buzzard from a small golden eagle.

He'd spent the last fortnight on something that was more a rock than an island, a fly-speck on maps of the Western Isles that could be described as dry land only on those rare days when it didn't rain. Though it was now officially summer, Philip had been wet so often that the contents of his backpack smelled of mould. In that fortnight he hadn't seen another human being. There had been him, the bird book and the birds squawking, quacking, bickering, and crapping on his one-man tent. It was heaven.

But all good things come to an end, and yesterday a boat had picked him up and returned him to—well; not, in the event, to civilization. He'd driven out of Oban and into trouble.

Now he was on the run. An essentially ordinary man, an engineer and a birder, he was embarrassed even to think in such terms, but that's what it amounted to. There were people hunting him, and half of them would like to see him dead and the other half wanted him behind bars. He needed to vanish for a while. Near Birmingham was the small Black Country town of Skipley where his sister lived.

If Mrs Mackey had been at home he'd have confided in her. But she and Ian were at a family wedding today, wouldn't be back till late, and there was no one else in the house. Two of the other tenants were teachers, they'd be back about five; the third was a solicitor's clerk who usually went for a drink after work. He'd see them all at breakfast in the morning, before he caught the InterCity. He'd be safe here for one night, surely.

Though he'd put a first-class stamp on his postcard he knew he might arrive on his sister's doorstep before it did. If she couldn't put him up he'd find a bed and breakfast. He wasn't sure what he ought to do next, only that he'd be better out of Edinburgh while he thought about it. At least the office weren't expecting him back for another fortnight. But he probably ought to phone the police.

He should, by rights, have phoned his sister. But Fee would be full of questions which he didn't feel up to answering just yet. By

4

tomorrow his mind would be clearer and he'd welcome her opinion. Fee could always be counted on for an opinion; at least one.

The window rattled again, the summer gale threatening the glass. Outside the walled garden, the closest thing Edinburgh had to a rain-forest, tossed like a green sea, and rain driving out of the leaden sky blotted up the afternoon sun so that he had lit the lamp on his desk. Mrs Mackey had given him her ground-floor room, thinking that a man who spent so much of his time outdoors would get claustrophobic upstairs. In fine weather he could wedge the window open and have direct access to the garden.

But not in weather like this. Philip turned his back on it and looked at his pack. He'd taken the tent out and exchanged the damp underwear and T-shirts for dry ones. It never occurred to him that a man of thirty-two really needed a different wardrobe for visiting his sister in the Midlands from what served for sitting on a rock in that great arm of the sea known as the Minch.

He glanced at his watch. He didn't know the time of the last collection but if Fee didn't get the card tomorrow morning she'd come home from school to find him sitting on his bag in her porch. If that happened, taken aback as she'd be it might take her, oh, ten or fifteen minutes to start telling him what to do next.

And he didn't know what he wanted to do

next. There were important issues at stake, but the fight wasn't his and he wouldn't have chosen to get involved. But though he wouldn't have picked sides, sides had been picked for him: if his life really was in danger he would have to go to the police. He just wished he could have been left out of it. He still half hoped that if he got out of Edinburgh, out of Scotland, it would all just blow over.

He reached for his anorak hanging behind the door; and then the window really did break under the hammer of the storm, glass tinkling to the floor beside the desk, the heavy curtain billowing into the room as the wind hit it like a fist. He pulled it aside to inspect the damage and shards of glass caught in the plush pricked his palm.

But the little rush of sound that escaped him then, half a grunt and half a gasp, had nothing to do with pain and the start of blood. There was someone outside, a man framed by the casement's jagged glass.

For some moments he regarded Philip and Philip regarded him in speculative silence. The storm hadn't broken the window: that was the man outside, and the light from the desk glinted off the thing in his right hand that he'd done it with.

Philip was an engineer, more familiar with spanners than guns, but developing the Third World had given him a liberal education and he knew that far and away the best thing you could

6

do in this situation was nothing. He stood still and waited for the other man to speak.

Eventually he did. 'Come with me. Bring your gear.'

Philip opened the casement and passed his backpack through. But as he went to follow, the man indicated the desk. 'Write your landlady a note. "Urgent business—back in a few weeks. Sorry about the window." Show me. Yes. Leave her twenty pounds.'

Philip did as he was told. But he didn't have twenty pounds—he'd been planning on using a cashpoint on the way to the station tomorrow. The man outside gave a rough little chuckle and passed him the note, and Philip wedged it together with the message under the edge of the lamp. As he did so, his hands screened by his body, he closed the book. When Mrs Mackey went to put it away—she was always putting his books away—she'd find the card. With any luck she'd post it.

The man said, 'Come now.' So Philip Morris went; and vanished, and was not for some time missed.

CHAPTER ONE

Another place, another time. Another desk, this one in an office, and behind it a tall slender woman of about thirty, her long brown hair bound up in a French plait, her large brown eyes lustrous. In her suit of willow-green twill, cut with an exquisite severity, the ambivalent colour a perfect foil for her flawless skin, she was a sight to strike terror into the hearts of working women everywhere. It's no longer enough for Superwoman merely to run the office, ran the unspoken message, she has to look *this good* doing it! And this was a sight that working women everywhere, or at least everywhere in the Midlands, would get the chance to see, captured as it was by the lens of a television camera.

It wasn't a big office so the cameraman was wedged in one corner while the interviewer perched on a chair in the open door. Behind her, though she'd already been shooed away twice, loomed Ms Holland's personal assistant Alex Fisher. At least, personal assistant was how she introduced herself. She made terrible coffee and worse jokes, and interrupted the proceedings with a raucous cackle of a laugh; but if there was no other reason for employing her the obvious one was good enough. The woman behind the desk would not have

9

seemed half so flawless, half so elegant, to someone who had not been shown in by a receptionist with all the personal charm of a brickie's labourer.

Conducting the interview was the bubbly Sally Vincent, who had two outstanding qualities as a broadcast journalist. One was the ability to seem bright and interested at the end of a long day, the other a precise instinct for timing. She knew, even allowing for out-takes, when she should be winding up. She glanced at the *Skipley Chronicle* lying open on the desk and the photograph of Primrose Holland gazed serenely back. '*The Primrose Path*—was that your idea or your editor's?'

The woman behind the desk elevated a shapely eyebrow in a tiny self-deprecating shrug. 'I don't remember now. It seemed appropriate for a feature of this type.'

'There *are* no other features of this type,' smiled Sally Vincent. 'Other newspapers may have agony aunts but style-wise this is a totally new departure. Which is why, of course, it's proving so popular. How does it feel to be the star of the year's most improbable media hit?'

'I'm not the star of anything,' demurred Ms Holland. 'If *The Primrose Path* has caught the public imagination it's because those who've written in have been decent, genuine people readers could identify with and care about, and their problems real dilemmas not easily resolved with tea and sympathy. They're the

10

stars of *The Primrose Path*. It would be impossible to write an interesting column if the only advice I could give was "Stop being so pathetic. This is the only life you're guaranteed, get on and live it!" '

'I'm sure that's true,' nodded Sally. 'But you do have an approach all your own. For instance'—she shuffled the cuttings in front of her—'Doris from Kidderminster was contemplating suicide as the only way out of a marriage to a man who'd abused her verbally, physically and sexually for twenty years. Do you remember your reply?'

The lustrous brown gaze dropped; Ms Holland had the grace to look faintly embarrassed. 'Um—'

'Did you tell her to call the Samaritans? Refer her to Women's Aid or the Rape Crisis Centre? Did you recommend the power of prayer and wish her the strength to bear it for the sake of the children?'

'Not exactly . . .'

'No. I have here what you wrote.' Sally Vincent was enjoying herself. ' "Buy or borrow a pair of wellies and a flat hat. Perfume your oldest anorak with sheep-dip. Chewing a straw, present yourself at your local police station and enquire about the procedure for taking out a shotgun licence. On no account mention being a battered wife . . ." '

When the television crew had left, the woman in the willow-green suit rising to see

11

them out, the sturdy receptionist threw herself into the chair behind the desk and let out a gale of magpie laughter. Tears were streaming down her plump cheeks by the time the younger woman returned.

She closed the door discreetly behind her before starting to shout. 'Rosie Holland, if you do anything like that to me ever again I shall— I shall—' Inspiration failed her. 'I don't know, but it'll be something awful!'

Struggling for breath, Rosie gasped moistly, 'Alex, you were wonderful! You're much better at being me than I am.'

'Even were that true,' snapped Alex, whose syntax did not desert her even under stress, 'it's beside the point. We were lying. We were lying, on camera, for a programme that'll be watched by thousands of people. We'll end up with egg all over our faces!'

Rosie blew her nose. She used men's handkerchiefs for the perfectly good reason that it was, to all intents and purposes, a man's nose. 'I don't see why. It's your photograph on the page, after all, and anyone who knows either of us knows that. Nobody's blown our cover yet.'

'I knew that was a terrible idea when I agreed to it.' Enervated, Alex sank on to the edge of the desk. 'I knew I'd regret it.'

'Nonsense,' Rosie said briskly, 'it was the only thing that made sense. We couldn't put my photograph on it—I have to be able to visit people without the neighbours immediately guessing they're Susy from Selly Oak. And it was your boyfriend who wanted a face on the page.'

'Matt Gosling is not my boyfriend!' Alex exclaimed indignantly, for all the world as if it were the first time she'd heard the rumour. 'He is my employer, as he is yours.'

''Course he is, Alex,' said Rosie in the tone of the deeply unconvinced. 'Anyway, it's not lying to use a professional name.'

'But you're not using a professional name, are you? You're using my face. And making me pretend to be you in front of a television camera!'

When Rosie Holland shrugged it was not a delicate evocative gesture like Alex's. It was more like one buffalo suggesting to another buffalo that it pursue its business elsewhere. 'Alex, we're a partnership: we use our ideas, my name and your face. That's not dishonest, it's business. You have the sort of face that sells newspapers. I have the sort of face that sells forklift trucks.'

Alex couldn't help smiling at that. It wasn't true, her contribution was more than secretarial but fell short of even a junior partnership, but it was typical of Rosie not only to say but to mean it. There was so much to like about the woman it was impossible to stay mad at her long enough for it to do some good. Alex sniffed, got up from the desk and, shaking her

13

head in mute despair, headed for the coffee machine.

Alex Fisher was perhaps the only person at the *Chronicle* who fed it money. Everyone else used a method pioneered by Rosie involving a sharp kick.

Much of the building was like the coffee machine, old and unpredictable. Away from the smarter public areas there were brick walls, some with the Victorian gas-lights still in place. The cellar was supposed to be haunted by a printer whose party-piece was putting his head in the paper guillotine.

The *Skipley Chronicle* was never one of the top newspapers in the Birmingham conurbation, though it was among the oldest. It began as a weekly in the nineteenth century, with advertisements for miracle soap and patent medicines on the front page and multiple strap headings that contained as much information and took up more space than the stories beneath. By the First World War it was publishing twice a week and the adverts on the front page were for motorcars and household appliances.

Skipley people valued their independence from the big city next door, and having their own newspaper underpinned it. For four years in the thirties the *Chronicle* came out as a daily, but newsprint restrictions in the Second World War ended that. The bi-weekly format, resumed as a stop-gap, continued for the next

14

twenty-two years, after which it went weekly again. By 1970 it was on the brink of closure.

But it was a family firm and the owners preferred to divert profits from more successful investments to keep it afloat. An uneasy equilibrium survived until the last of the family died in 1992, when the paper passed to a second cousin in Australia who put it up for sale, either as a going concern or a town-centre building site.

'Can I help?' As Alex turned away, the machine grumbling abdominally over the unfamiliar meal of money, two plastic cups sloshing in one hand as she wedged her purse under her elbow, a third and larger hand materialized by her shoulder.

'Oh, thanks, Matt,' she said, letting him take the cups. 'Are you coming in? Rosie's dying to tell someone how clever she's been.' She felt in her purse for another coin.

Matt Gosling shook his head sadly, gave her back the two cups and obtained a third by rattling the machine with a kick like a mule's. He was a big man; also, one of his feet didn't bruise in the usual way.

He had only one qualification to be a newspaper proprietor. He'd never worked in the industry. He was a soldier until he left his lower right leg in the wreckage of an armoured car outside Newry. He'd never run a business of any sort. He was still on crutches when he came to Skipley and at that time the *Chronicle*

15

building had no lifts. But he had seen *Citizen Kane*. He too thought it would be fun to run a newspaper.

In the space of about two months Gosling had bought the *Chronicle*, scrapped the old rotary presses, negotiated a time-share deal on a web-offset array in Birmingham and put in a lift. Then he set about updating the content. Adverts were evicted from the front page around 1950: now Gosling banned the wedding photographs that had replaced them. He demoted star pupils of local dancing teachers to the inside as well. And the annual concert of the Gilbert & Sullivan Society. And the Pigeon Club's monthly champion. 'To the bulk of our readers,' he told an affronted club secretary, 'one pigeon looks very much like another.'

He hired new staff capable of replacing dancing tots and pouting pigeons with something better. An editor who knew that while a local weekly shouldn't try to compete with the nationals it should deliver real news, properly researched, intelligently written and attractively laid out. Also a photographer who hadn't learned his trade taking mug-shots for Winson Green prison, and a women's page editor. From the outset that was always going to be either the best decision he made or the worst.

Rosie Holland was working as a pathologist in a West Country hospital. For light relief, and because she didn't get a lot of feed-back from

16

her patients, she wrote a health column for a Bristol paper, which was how the *Chronicle*'s new editor Dan Sale knew of her. It wasn't the sort of health column usually seen in the provinces—asked about emergency contraception she wrote: 'The word No, enunciated clearly and repeated often enough, will prevent most pregnancies'—and Sale imagined her doing something similarly breezy for the *Chronicle*, faxing him her contribution each week.

He'd have been wise to discuss it with her himself; but he was busy and Matt offered to go instead. He met Rosie at her hospital and they went for a three-hour lunch; the same day she handed in her notice and put her house up for sale. She hadn't realized how dull her life had become until the man with the tin leg limped into her morgue.

She saw a young man of twenty-nine, tall and strongly built, still trying to walk like a soldier though he had yet to achieve either physical or psychological comfort with his prosthesis. Months of illness had stripped his skin of colour: he looked pasty and drawn, light brown hair glued to his broad forehead by the effort of walking from the carpark, a distance that a year ago he'd have sprinted without breaking sweat. But beneath the pallor Rosie glimpsed the bones of something strong and enduring. Ten years of his life were etched on his face too deeply to be entirely erased by what had

17

happened.

Three months before his transport drove over a culvert with a bomb in it Lieutenant Matt Gosling made captain; but since he'd done it primarily by being fitter and faster than any of his soldiers he surprised no one by spending less time in the office than any captain the company could remember. He was the last man who should have been crippled, and family and friends worried how he'd cope.

But soldiers know about disability, never see a crutch or a white stick without thinking that could be them. When it happened to Matt he coped by throwing all his energy first into getting well and then into making a new career not dependent on being able to run a mile in full kit. The bomb had left much more than it had taken and the determination to succeed was like silver bullets in the glance of his pale blue eyes. Rosie's first thought was: If I were ten years younger!

Though she was aware that, even ten years ago, she was not an irresistible magnet to handsome young men. She'd been thirty-seven, five foot eight and fourteen stone, with brown hair that frizzed at the threat of rain and a crooked front tooth where she'd broken up a brawl in Accident & Emergency. She smoked too much, drank too much and swore like a trooper. With eyes like that, even a one-legged man could do better.

So she might have been surprised to know

the impact she had had on Matt Gosling: not even so much as a woman, more as a force of nature. He felt himself to be in the presence of an Immortal: Gaia, the Earth Mother, the Willendorf Venus, the Sphinx. Working up to her elbows in the formaldehyde stink of death she was the very stuff of life, her wide face and red cheeks aglow with health, her brown eyes sharp with intelligent good humour, her big deft hands hunting disaster down all the labyrinthine ways of the human body. An amalgam in one monolithic form of every school matron, every regimental sergeant-major and every buxom barmaid he'd ever met.

Over lunch at a nearby pub Matt talked—at length, he rather suspected, and with excessive enthusiasm—about his plans for the *Chronicle*, and the more he talked the more discontented Rosie became with an existence that hadn't changed in any material way for fifteen years. Financially she was secure; she had no dependants to consider or consult; before the new media mogul had even offered her a job she was spelling out her terms and conditions.

'I'm not interested in writing an essay in first-year medicine every week,' she warned. 'I want a staff job. I want a page, and a broad degree of freedom as to what I fill it with.'

Matt could have refused her nothing. 'Such as—?'

'Well, health matters, of course. Ailment of the week, news on medicine and surgery,

19

maybe a *Good Drug Guide*—some are worse than the diseases they're prescribed for. All the latest surveys showing that eating, drinking and being merry are better for you than being careful.' She gave her infectious cackle of a laugh, dumped ketchup on her burger. 'I'm particularly keen on those. And . . .'

'What?'

'How about an advice column? Partly medical, partly help for the troubled and lovelorn. Can you see me as an Agony Aunt?' But before he could reply she'd forged ahead. 'Something a bit gutsier than the usual. I don't arse around, you know.' Matt had never thought for a moment that she might. 'If people need telling to extract the digit that's what I'll say. What do you think—worth the risk?' She gave a huge Cheshire-cat grin.

He didn't want time to think about it or even discuss it with Dan Sale. 'Yes,' he said simply.

So he had some explaining to do when he got back to Skipley. But it was too late to back out, even if he'd been prepared to. Rosie Holland was on her way and the *Skipley Chronicle* would never be the same again.

Alex came with her. Rosie needed a secretary and Alex had run the chief administrator's office at the hospital. For two such different women they got on well and Rosie needed someone who could stand up to her if need be.

Alex could never quite remember why she'd

20

thrown up a good job for something about as permanent as a chocolate teapot. It wasn't the money: Matt did his best but couldn't match what she'd left at the hospital. It must have been that contagious enthusiasm spreading from Matt to Rosie to her, like scabies.

Matt Gosling. Of course, she'd heard the gossip. It was unfounded. Certainly she liked him. He was a kind, brave, admirable man; it would be perverse not to like him. She hoped he liked her. But Alex had two inflexible rules about dating: she didn't go out with married men, and she didn't date people from work. If her employer needed a partner for an official function, or secretarial assistance at a weekend meeting, or if she and Rosie and Matt and Dan Sale had an evening at the theatre or met for Sunday lunch at a country pub, that was different. That wasn't dating, it was just four single people—Dan was a widower—doing things together instead of doing them alone. There was nothing between Alex Fisher and Matt Gosling but a friendly professional relationship.

Now the *Chronicle* had been under new management for fifteen months and Rosie Holland had been there for six. *The Primrose Path*—the name had in fact been chosen in a dyspeptic moment by Dan, who thought he'd never met anyone less like a Primrose than his new women's page editor—had been an instant success, the circulation had doubled and Matt

21

Gosling had graduated from crutches to a stick to a heavy limp to really quite a jaunty one.

Rosie, still chuckling over the morning's sport, drank her coffee, her fourth since getting in at nine, then reached for her coat. 'Who's coming to lunch?'

Alex cast a startled eye at her watch. 'At five past twelve?'

Rosie shrugged. 'So we'll have a drink first. Come on, there's nothing to do here for a bit. Have you looked at the in-tray?'

'Of course.' Alex sounded quite affronted. She read all the mail as soon as it came up from the front desk.

'The highlight of that lot is some woman who wants Interpol to investigate why she hasn't had a postcard from her brother. I'm off down The Spotted Ferret for a ploughman's. Maybe there'll be a nice juicy sexual fantasy waiting when we get back.'

CHAPTER TWO

Alex answered the phone on the third ring, which was what she aimed at. Longer than that smacked of inefficiency; sooner suggested you'd nothing better to do than hover over it.

'Is that the advice column?' It was a man's voice, but that was not unusual. Women and girls accounted for the majority of calls and letters but perhaps one in four were from men.

'How can I help you?'

'Slugs,' said the man on the phone. There was a subcurrent of desperation in his voice and he didn't give her the chance to refer him to the gardening page. 'Do they come in different varieties?'

Eight years in a hospital had taught Alex never to be surprised; working on *The Primrose Path* had elevated that to an art form. She racked her memory for information. 'I believe so. There are those big grey field slugs that are like stepping on a skateboard. Then there's the little black one.'

Interest quickened at the other end of the line. 'How little?'

Alex squinted at the phone. 'If it matters, maybe you should ask a garden centre. At a guess I'd say three or four centimetres. They look like a bit of liquorice.'

'Or a blackcurrant jelly baby?'

'Well yes, I suppose—' Premonition stopped her mid-sentence.

'Oh shit!' said the man on the phone. 'Shit shit shit shit shit.' The instrument went dead.

People phoned, or wrote, or occasionally called in. As Rosie came through reception there was a girl at the front desk asking to see her.

'I'm Rosie Holland. Come on upstairs, tell me what the problem is.'

But the girl didn't fall obediently into step behind her. 'What I have to say won't take that

23

long.' There was a hard note in her voice that made Rosie look again.

The girl was older than she'd thought, probably mid-twenties: small of stature, a cap of short fair hair and a pair of huge sapphire-blue eyes made her seem younger. She was wearing a long T-shirt and baggy shorts with a bum-bag strapped around her taut waist.

Rosie sighed. Penny from Harborne: I fancy my sister's new husband? Blossom from Handsworth: Mummy and Daddy still treat me like a child? Or perhaps—outside chance this but worth an each-way bet—Simon from Skipley West: Nobody here knows I'm gay. 'Should I know your name?'

'Fiona Morris. I wrote about finding my brother—he vanished after a camping trip. The police say if there are no suspicious circumstances it's none of their business if a grown man goes walkabout. I wondered how to go about finding a reputable private investigator.'

'Yes, I remember,' said Rosie. 'A teacher, was he?' There was nothing in it for the column. She'd replied briefly by letter and forgotten about it.

Fiona Morris breathed heavily. 'I'm the teacher; Philip's an engineer. He got back from the Persian Gulf in May and went for a fortnight's bird-watching in the Hebrides. On the first of June he was home again, for just one day apparently: he left word he'd be away a bit

24

longer and vanished off the globe. Last week, when he'd been gone six weeks and I still hadn't had a card, I wrote to you.'

'And I replied,' Rosie said patiently, 'didn't I?'

'If you want to call it that.' The girl's lips were tight. 'I'm worried sick Philip's come to some harm, and you reckon he's getting his rocks off in a tartan knocking-shop and I'll hear from him when he needs his fare home!'

'That's not what I said!' Rosie exclaimed indignantly. Then, remembering: 'Not in so many words.'

She'd written: 'I expect your brother spotted some Highland beauty the first time he raised his binoculars and they've yet to come up for air. My guess is you'll hear from him in three months, asking you to send him money, or in twelve asking you to be godmother to twins.'

'It was the words', said Fee Morris forcibly, 'that I found so offensive! Who the hell do you think you're dealing with—some apprentice hairdresser whose idea of a really big adventure is a week in Benidorm? Between us my brother and I have lived in, worked in, or crossed two-thirds of the world's surface. He builds bridges in Africa and dams in Arabia; I've taught English in a Brazilian slum. We don't spend every waking minute worrying about one another's safety!'

'Then why this time?' Rosie was aware of having misread the situation. She'd pictured

25

Miss Morris as a staid, conventional, middle-aged schoolma'am getting hysterical about a man sowing his wild oats. Meeting the girl, Rosie began to wonder if she'd been too quick to dismiss her concern.

'Because there was no postcard.' In spite of what she'd said Fee did want to talk about it, and allowed Rosie to usher her upstairs. 'It's a kind of tradition: everywhere we go we send a card. This is where I am now, third mud hut from the right, next week I'm moving up-country, I'll write again then. Always—however inconvenient. I got a card from Oban, which was the last post-box before he went out to his bird-infested rock in the Western Isles, but that's nine weeks ago. So far as I can discover, nobody's heard from him for seven. He's never been out of touch so long.'

They reached the office. Alex cleared some papers off a chair so the visitor could sit down. 'Perhaps he sent a card and it never arrived,' said Rosie.

The girl's expression was scathing. 'Credit me with some intelligence, Ms Holland! That was my first thought too—he's on top of a Scottish mountain and a sheep ate the mail. So I called his landlady and his office, and neither of them knew where he was or why he wasn't back long before now. It's so unlike him to let people down. I even tried the Edinburgh police—he lives in Edinburgh. They were polite enough but they said that without blood

26

on the carpet there was nothing they could do. They said he was probably fine, he'd just got tired of his job, he'd turn up again soon.

'But I don't believe it. Philip loves his job; and he loves me—he wouldn't worry me like this if he'd any choice. So whatever the police think, something has happened to him. I want to hire a private detective. I hoped you could point me towards someone honest. I didn't,' she added with asperity, 'need telling that boys will be boys and it's nothing for me to worry my pretty little head about. I expect that crap from men, I didn't expect it from you.'

Rosie gave an apologetic sniff. 'Sorry about that. Going off what you told me it seemed reasonable enough.' She paused, her nose wrinkled in thought. 'What is it you think might have happened? That you're afraid of?'

Fee blinked. 'Afraid's too big a word. Isn't it?'

'You've gone to a lot of trouble for someone who's only puzzled and irritated. If I thought my brother was in so much trouble that he couldn't even call me, damn sure I'd be afraid.'

After a moment Fee nodded. 'You're right. But I don't know what can have gone wrong. If he'd had an accident the police would know. What else can have happened to a civil engineer and bird-watcher?'

Rosie thought, then she shook her head. 'I don't think you need a private detective. What could he do that you can't? It's summer, you're

27

a teacher: why not look for him yourself?'

Taken aback, Fee's sapphire eyes flared. 'I wouldn't know where to start!'

'A private eye would only know what you could tell him. Let's see. You know Philip was in Edinburgh on the first of June. He got back from a bird-watching trip and left word that he was going to be a bit longer. Maybe he went back to the same place.'

'I thought of that. I called the piermaster in Oban. He remembered Philip coming back at the end of May—he sent a boat for him—but he hadn't seen him since.'

'So he fancied a change of birds. Where else might he have gone?'

'Have you never been to Scotland?' asked the girl in amazement. 'There's a lot of it. And in most of it, birds is all there is.'

'OK, so we have to narrow it down. Does he belong to any bird-watching societies that might know where he went?'

Fee looked chastened. 'I never thought of that. I'll ask the landlady to send me his address book. There might be a club in there. If necessary I'll work through all his friends, see which of them are bird-watchers too.'

'I know a bird-watcher,' Rosie remembered suddenly. 'I even know a bird-watcher who lived for forty years in the Western Highlands. He might know some people we could call. Leave me your phone number. I'll ring you when I've talked to him.'

'All right. Thanks. And'—Fee hesitated, embarrassed—'I'm sorry I snapped at you. I've been worried. I was looking for someone to take it out on.'

Rosie beamed expansively. 'That's what I'm here for.'

When the girl had gone Alex frowned. 'Who do you know who used to live in the Western Highlands?'

Rosie rocked a strong-fingered hand. 'All right, so I don't *know* him. But I know *of* someone, and so do you. He's in your file, early on—not the first week's *Path* but maybe the second or third. Purbright? Parsons? Something like that. He wrote in about noisy neighbours, said he'd spent the last forty years teaching in Argyll . . .'

His name was Arthur Prufrock and his letter, regurgitated by Alex's meticulous filing system, was redolent of pipe tobacco and the swish of a well-polished cane.

After teaching for forty years at a small private school in Argyll I retired two years ago and, aware that the Scottish winters were beginning to play havoc with my joints, returned to my native West Midlands. It was not an easy decision—my main pleasure for most of my life has been walking the moors with binoculars in one hand and *Birds of Britain* in the other—but the surrounding countryside has much to offer the

29

ornithologist and until four months ago I had no regrets.

Since then, however, I have been disturbed most nights by the domestic disharmony and curious musical tastes of the family renting the adjoining house. I spent my career turning young ruffians into gentlemen and am not prepared to tolerate deliberate bad manners in my own home; but polite remonstrance got me nowhere, and a young friend warns that blowing off their chimney pot with a 12-bore would be frowned on by the police. I'm reluctant to involve the authorities in such a trivial matter. Your advice would be appreciated.

*   *   *

'Which was what?' said Rosie. 'Remind me.'

Alex had appended a clipping to the foot of the letter.

The 12-bore sounds good to me too, but you'd probably end up in court charged with malicious damage and unlawfully discharging a firearm. The duty of keeping the peace rests with the police, and the local authority Environmental Health Department has an obligation to deal with actionable nuisances under Sections 79 and 80 of the Environmental Protection Act of 1990.

While you're waiting for them to implement an abatement notice you could vent your frustrations on the owner or agent for the property—nobody likes getting a roasting over tenants—and ease your discomfort by masking the row with something more congenial of your own. A loud noise a little way off may be covered by quite soft music close at hand. Experiment with different sounds to see what works best—Mozart, Wagner, a relaxation tape, stags bellowing on Ben Nevis . . . You'll find it pleasanter than World War III next door, and it may enable you to sleep through the racket.

A final thought. If you go to bed earlier than next door, perhaps you wake up earlier, too. If so I would suggest that first thing in the morning would be an ideal time to vacuum, cut the lawn, play Fetch with the dog, brush up your bagpipes technique, whatever.

'Give him a call,' said Rosie. 'Ask when he'll be at home. Tell him I have a problem I needhis help with.'

*   *   *

Twenty years dissecting the consequences of other people's errors had not improved Rosie's driving but had taught her that when a bad driver meets a good driver the one in the biggest car comes off best. She drove a 4x4

31

Korean estate that was essentially a tank with upholstery.

After a couple of false turns she found the row of red-brick two-storey cottages in Foxford Lane, at the back of the steep rise west of Skipley known as The Brink. Outside one of the cottages, Rosie noted with satisfaction, hung a To Let sign.

Skipley, though of no more than moderate size and often derided by the big city next door as Skimpy, was essentially industrial, a manufacturing and commercial centre, a town of businessmen and shopkeepers. Where Birmingham had modernized ruthlessly, ending up with nothing more distinctive than a nightmare motorway junction, Skipley had stuck with its Victorian roots, many of its Victorian buildings and much of the Victorian soot still clinging to them.

Foxford, on the other hand, was rural, a reminder of the old Midlands landscape of farms and villages predating even the soot. When these red-brick cottages were built, one would almost certainly have housed a carter's family, one a blacksmith, and one an old woman who taught small children in her front room and made toffee on a nail in the kitchen door.

There was a vehicle already parked in the lane, Rosie noted: an elderly Land Rover, the sober green livery turned to a pirate motley by the panels which had been begged, borrowed or salvaged to replace damaged ones and never painted to match. One door was orange, one cream, and a man was lifting a cylinder mower into the back. As Rosie passed he growled, 'Half an hour, at the end of the lane.'

If Alex had been there she'd have hurried on, knowing better than to talk to strange men, let alone very strange ones; but Rosie came about like a wind-jammer changing tack. 'Are you propositioning me?'

The man blinked, as people suddenly confronted with Rosie Holland tended to. Then he scowled. 'You asked the time of the next bus.'

'No,' said Rosie, 'I didn't.'

The voice, which would have been deep even without the growl, and the glower suggested a man in the throes of a grumpy middle-age. But he was actually much younger than that, which didn't make his bad manners any worse but did make them harder to forgive. Rosie thought being in your mid-twenties was all the excuse anyone needed to sing, whistle and grin like an idiot all day.

Instead, heavy brows lowered over deep-set eyes in which smouldered an anger he made no effort to disguise though Rosie could not possibly have provoked it. One corner of his lip lifted in a snarl. 'Suit yourself.' He slammed the back of the vehicle, clambered in at the orange door and drove away, spitting gravel at her from under the broad wheels.

Rosie watched in amazement. 'I hope your

exhaust falls off *and* a police car runs over it!'
Then she shrugged off the whole absurd
episode and looked along the row for
Prufrock's address.

There was nothing to distinguish No. 5 from
those around it. They all had pocket-
handkerchief front lawns and roses round the
door, and shared a long fuchsia hedge with
little wicket gates. Under the canopy of roses
the front door was closing.

Rosie let out a bellow they must have heard
at Spaghetti Junction and, putting on a
surprising turn of speed for so substantial a
woman, swung in at the gate.

Thanks to Alex's phone call Arthur Prufrock
was not shocked into fibrillation by the sound
of his name issuing from a human megaphone.
He opened the door again and stood waiting on
the step, a cautious smile of welcome turning to
a puzzled frown. 'Miss Holland?'

'Ms,' she corrected him automatically.
'Rosie Holland. Nice to meet you.'

He shook her hand politely, his own almost
disappearing in the clinch. He was not a big
man: the boys at his school had called him
Prudence, though not in his hearing. Forty
years on a Scottish hill had barely weathered
him: his skin glowed and the little white
moustache bristled with energy. A fringe of
white hair threw a halo around his pink skull
and his eyes were the colour of ice on
periwinkles. He was a few years short of

34

seventy. 'Arthur Prufrock.' The first creak of age was audible in his voice. 'I'm sorry, I didn't recognize you.'

'It's not my photograph on the page,' Rosie admitted cheerfully. 'It's my assistant's, Alex Fisher—you spoke on the phone. She's the public face of *The Primrose Path*: I'm the portrait in her attic.'

Under the white moustache Prufrock's smile broadened. 'It was you who answered my query, though. That surprised me. I couldn't equate the tone of that with the picture.'

Rosie arched an interrogative eyebrow. 'You're an astute man, Mr Prufrock.'

'And you're a wise woman, Miss Holland. I took your advice.' He nodded at the To Let board next door. 'As you see, it worked.'

Rosie nodded. 'Not as satisfying as the 12-bore but probably better in the long run.'

'Come in. How can I help you?'

The living room he showed her into was filled to the low-beamed ceiling with photographs of Scottish birds. If he took them himself he must have risked life and limb on a regular basis. Admittedly some of the most spectacular were in black and white, suggesting that he hadn't clambered eighty feet up a bare rock crag to get that shot of a peregrine falcon on her nest in the last few years. But others were in full colour and obviously taken with good modern equipment. The quality was superb.

Apart from the photographs, the room was

much what you would have expected of an elderly schoolmaster living alone: scrupulously clean and irredeemably old-fashioned. There were antimacassars on the chairs and a lace cloth on the dining table. There was also a tray with cups and a pot on it. Prufrock took it into the kitchen. 'I'll make some more.'

The significance of that was not lost on Rosie. 'The lout outside—he was here? Who is he?'

Prufrock looked at her over his moustache as he might have looked at a pupil offering a minor impertinence. 'My gardener, and the friend I mentioned—the one who warned against taking the law into my own hands. Why do you call him a lout?'

Rosie repeated what had passed between them. 'Why was he so angry? He looked at me as if I'd thrown his baby off a train.'

Prufrock smiled drily. 'It wasn't you he was angry with, it was me. We had words. He said I could clip my own expletive-deleted topiary in future and went off in a huff.'

'He got that upset over a hedge?'

'Oh no. We were talking—' He stopped abruptly then, his gaze growing speculative. 'Ah. Yes, you're rather good at this, aren't you?'

'At what?' asked Rosie innocently.

'At getting people to open up, to trust you. But you didn't come here to discuss my gardener. What is it you think I can help with?'

He listened with his pink hands pressed

36

together and his ice-blue eyes turned up as if to ethereal music. In all the world, Rosie thought, he could only have been two things: a country parson or a teacher in a minor public school. And now the parson would wear a beard, ride a motorbike and hold a rave in the aisle after confirmations.

When he had all the meagre details Prufrock looked pensively at an eagle soaring over the fireplace. 'And all you know is that he might be watching birds in Scotland? That'll be like looking for an egg on a pebble beach.'

Rosie nodded apologetically. 'I wondered if there was anything going on that a bird nut would change the habits of a lifetime for.'

'There's always something of interest to somebody. But from what you say he isn't a twitcher.' Seeing Rosie's confusion Prufrock explained. 'It's a term of abuse in ornithology circles—twitchers dash hither and yon to see the latest bird in much the way that young girls go round looking at pop singers, just so they can say they've seen them. A tick in the notebook and they're off looking for the next. But you say Mr Morris would sit on the same rock for days or even weeks. That's more like a scientific survey and would probably be organized by a society. I'll phone round, try to find who he was working for.'

Rosie was happy with that. 'If we can even whittle down the time he's been missing—if somebody can put him on Skye in the second week of June, say—it'll give his sister some idea where to start looking.'

'I hope I can justify your confidence in me, Miss Holland,' he said.

'Ms,' said Rosie.

'Bless you,' said Prufrock politely.

He walked her out to her car; partly, no doubt, because it was the correct thing to do, but also because he was curious. Rosie didn't understand why.

The white moustache twitched. 'Let's just say that if Shad Lucas had told me the time of the next bus I'd want to make sure my car would start.'

Rosie was still pondering that, Prufrock holding the gate for her, when her face froze and then melted with uncharacteristic uncertainty. Prufrock looked where she was staring.

The car canted as if she'd parked it half on the kerb. But there wasn't a kerb, and though the lane was a bit rough-and-ready she'd have noticed if she'd had to climb out uphill.

In the normal course of events Rosie Holland swore fully, freely and confidently. She swore affectionately at friends, amiably at colleagues, briskly at tradesmen and fulsomely at small children. But when she was really and genuinely startled she fell back on her father's preferred exclamation. 'I'll go to the foot of our stairs!'

The Korean tank had a flat tyre.

CHAPTER THREE

While Rosie changed the wheel Arthur Prufrock talked about his gardener.

He did, of course, offer to help with the wheel. But Rosie was both younger and stronger, and suspected she'd manage better without him. He looked at the tool-kit as if he only knew the spanner through a friend of a friend and didn't recognize the wheelbrace at all. He watched in horrid fascination as she jacked up the car.

'Your gardener', said Rosie, cranking steadily, 'is psychic?'

'Do you know, I'm not sure?' said Prufrock. 'I've given it a lot of thought and I'm still not sure what he is. He knows things, can do things most of us can't, but whether that makes him psychic I honestly couldn't say.'

'What kind of things?'

'Well, he's a dowser. In itself that's nothing remarkable. Lots of people can dowse for water. Shad can find more than water but maybe that just makes him a better dowser rather than something else. Psychic? I don't know.'

'What does he say?'

'Not very much. If I were to ask him how he knew about your tyre he'd say he must have heard the air escaping.'

'Maybe he did.'

'You didn't, and he was on the other side of

the lane.'

'Maybe I didn't have a puncture then. Maybe he came back after I went inside and drove a tin-tack into it.' She had the wheel off now and there it was, sunk deep in the tread designed to cope with a wet spring in Seoul. 'Not clairvoyance, not super-human hearing, just malice.'

Prufrock was chuckling into the moustache that had more personality than some people Rosie knew. 'Shad isn't the easiest company in the world. He lacks social skills. He's brusque with strangers, and shows a lamentable want of gratitude to those who take an interest in his life. But random acts of meanness?—no.'

'Then what are you saying? That he saw it in his crystal ball?'

'No, nothing that specific. But I do think he saw it coming. Nothing else makes sense. How many miles a year do you drive?'

Rosie didn't understand but answered anyway. 'Twelve, fifteen thousand?'

'And how many punctures do you get?'

'One? Not always that.'

'So the odds against you getting one here were astronomical. Can we at least agree that it wasn't a lucky guess?' Rosie considered, then nodded. 'And can you take my word that he isn't the kind of man who would deliberately drive a tack into your wheel?' She thought a little longer this time but finally nodded again. 'Then we're left with only two options: that his hearing is better than yours by a factor of four or more—and if he heard the air escaping why wouldn't he say so?—or that he has a sixth sense for which you and I have no equivalent. Which is what I think. I'm not sure that makes him psychic; I do think he's abnormally sensitive.'

Rosie lined up the new tyre and hefted it into place. Alex kept a set of white overalls in her car for this but she never had to use them: knights in shining armour queued up to help her. Rosie was used to managing alone, got on with the job without much concern for her clothes. A process akin to natural selection ensured that everything she owned was machine-washable: things that shrank or ran or felted were dumped in favour of those that didn't.

With a dusty black semi-circle printed on her front she straightened up and met the old man's gaze. 'A gardener with second sight. Now I've heard it all.'

Prufrock shrugged, and his eyes twinkled, and he said nothing more.

When the jack was back in the boot Rosie said, 'What were you arguing about?'

Prufrock frowned. 'Were we arguing?'

'You said he was angry with you.'

'Oh, yes.' He pursed his lips, the pink jowls falling into ready-made creases. 'The same thing, actually: whether his perception is random luck or something more, how long you

41

can go on calling it coincidence before it becomes downright absurd.'

Rosie didn't understand. 'But if you believe he can do it, why were you arguing?'

Impish crinkles appeared around the periwinkle eyes. 'Because Shad doesn't; or doesn't want to. He says there's nothing paranormal about making the odd lucky guess. He says everyone gets lucky sometimes and gets cross when I won't accept that as an adequate explanation. It happens too often to dismiss it like that. I want him to have it properly assessed. He says he's not going to turn himself into a freak show to satisfy my schoolgirl fantasies.'

'Which is when you threw him out.'

Prufrock shook his head. 'Which is when I gave him another cup of tea, a chocolate digestive biscuit and the address of the Society for Psychical Research. He accused me of meddling in his life, I asked after his mother and he stormed out.'

'His mother?' Rosie had had some surreal conversations in her time but this was world class.

The car was fixed, the business that had brought her here complete, but she could no more have left now than miss the last act of *Hamlet*. They continued the conversation over lamb cobbler in the nearest pub. Prufrock, who wasn't driving, had a sherry with his. Rosie cast covetous eyes along the row of optics behind the bar.

'Shad's mother is a gypsy. She reads tea-leaves in an end-of-the-pier show in Clacton or Southend or somewhere. Except that she doesn't. It's pure theatre. She's priceless as entertainment but about as psychic as a barrow-load of wet cement.' He was clearly quoting the gardener: DIY, like motor mechanics, was a closed book to Arthur Prufrock.

'A non-conductive medium,' murmured Rosie slyly, and Prufrock grinned. 'And Shad thinks that, because she can't do it, therefore he can't do it?'

'Not exactly. I think he knows that he can, and he's afraid of opening Pandora's box. Do you know anything about dowsing?'

'What, twigs and water and stuff?'

'That's it. It's so routine a phenomenon it's hardly considered paranormal. They say almost anyone can learn to do it. Shad learned as a boy, but a time came when it gave him some problems and he quit. Now he's afraid that if he opens the sluice again, what's built up behind it will sweep him away.'

'Why are you telling me this?' asked Rosie curiously. 'Do you want me to talk to him?'

Prufrock regarded her askance. 'You mean, since you had such a positive effect on one another the first time?' He shook his head. 'No. If he knew I'd been talking about him he'd resent it; and if he really did walk out on me,

43

there's a wisteria in the back garden that's big enough to move indoors, take over my best armchair and demand a say in what we watch on television. No, leave Shad to me, Miss Holland, at least for the moment. I'll be sure to ask if I think you can help.'

Rosie had given up trying to plant political correctness in such unpromising loam. She sighed. 'Call me Rosie.'

*   *   *

She had guests for supper that evening, sat Alex and Matt and Dan down in the kitchen while she worked. It was a big Victorian kitchen, designed with staff in mind. The house was built as a vicarage: it was too big for one woman living alone but Rosie loved its generous proportions.

In the kitchen was a long oak table. Dan Sale sat at one end, his wrinkled-walnut face all disbelief as Rosie told the story of the psychic gardener and the punctured tyre. 'Whatever the old man said, there's only one possibility,' he said when she finished. Thirty years as a newspaperman had left him with few illusions. 'He sneaked back after you'd gone inside and spiked it.'

'Why?' asked Rosie.

'He's young,' said Dan morosely, as if that explained everything. 'What more reason do you need?' Dan had a son. They hadn't

44

exchanged a civil word in a decade and a half.

'He deliberately punctured the tyre of someone he knew was visiting his employer?'

Sale shrugged. 'You said they'd been arguing.'

'Dan, if every time you argued with an employee he went out and let down someone's tyre, half the West Midlands would grind to a halt. However cross he was with Prufrock, why would he drive a tin-tack into my wheel?'

'What's the alternative? That he really can predict the future?' It was hard to judge from Matt Gosling's tone if he was open to the possibility or not. He was a good-natured man and that note of amused tolerance sometimes made people think he was a soft touch, a man who could be pushed around without pushing back. No one made the mistake twice.

'That's not what Prufrock said.' Rosie set a potluck casserole on the table. 'Not exactly. Not seeing the future the way you can see this casserole; perhaps picking up hints about it. If you were in the hall and heard me put something heavy on the table and smelled gravy, you might infer we were having some kind of stew. More that sort of thing.'

She saw from his expression that Dan was unconvinced and let out a gust of laughter. 'OK, then try this. You can hear a bus coming. You can feel a tube train coming, from the change in air pressure. What if all coming events cast a shadow before them which sufficiently well-tuned people can detect?

'Maybe that's what Prufrock means by sensitive, I'd mean by perceptive and you'd mean by canny. You've worked with a lot of reporters down the years. I bet you've known two or three who were always, but always, in the right place at the right time.' Head cocked, she challenged him to deny it.

Dan opened his mouth to do so, closed it again. Rosie crowed. 'See?'

'It's not the same thing,' objected Matt. 'There are soldiers like that, too, who *know* where the sniper's going to be, but that's not ESP. Mostly it's being natural snipers themselves—they know where they'd put themselves to command the field of fire. What you're talking about, someone who can predict random events, is more like a soldier saying "The sniper's going to be on that crest over there, and his name's George!"'

'So you reckon Prufrock was giving me a load of horse-feathers. That the puncture was either coincidence or malice, and on the spur of the moment Prufrock invented a pack of lies about a psychic gardener. That's even weirder than ESP!'

'But you're making it out to be black or white, and it isn't.' Matt enjoyed arguing with Rosie. It was a game of pure military tactics, like chess. 'Maybe he noticed the tack in your tyre. Maybe he heard the air escaping. Consciously or unconsciously, he knew you'd

46

got a problem and he was starting to tell you, only you jumped down his throat so fast he thought you were dangerous and got off-side. Admit it, Rosie, you do have that effect on people.'

'Me? Nah.' The twinkle in her eye was as close to an admission as he was likely to get. 'And I didn't jump down his throat. I was, as ever, the soul of sweet reason.' No one contradicted her, but the stunned silence did not imply consent so much as admiration at her impudence.

Despairing of getting her supper, Alex took over the ladle and began to serve. Against all expectations Rosie was a good plain cook: she didn't cut fancy shapes in vegetables but nobody left the table hungry. The casserole filled the kitchen with steam, rich smells and expectation. 'Anyway,' said Alex diplomatically, 'I don't suppose we'll ever know now.'

As soon as she'd said it she knew it was a mistake. The twinkle in Rosie's eye turned to a glitter. 'Alex, dear, how long have we known each other? Of course I shall know, because I shall find out.' Around the table the atmosphere shivered like a struck crystal in mingled hope and trepidation; much as it had in Rome two thousand years earlier when Julius Caesar leaned across the map of Europe and said, 'And what lies west of Gaul?'

CHAPTER FOUR

Alex approached the desk with a sheaf of papers and a severe expression. 'No, Rosie,' she said firmly.

'No what?' Rosie had a fairly good idea.

'No, you can't ask Dan to print that. He'll have a seizure and you'll be responsible for the death of a decent man and a good editor.'

Rosie took the copy off her, scanned it with the outrage of a mother who's been told her only-begotten has written Fuck in his hymn-book. 'What's wrong with it?'

The perfectly formed nostrils flared and Alex breathed tersely at her. 'You're not a pathologist any longer. Talking like that upsets people.'

'Like what?'

'Explicitly.'

'What—vagina?' Rosie started to grin.

'In that context,' Alex said stiffly, 'yes. And you should scrub the bit about the brother'. Straight-backed, she walked out.

When she'd gone, chuckling to herself, Rosie read both the letter—from Ruth who lived on The Brink—and her reply again.

Is my mother becoming a nymphomaniac?

A late change of plan meant I arrived home unexpectedly last Saturday night. I thought my mother would be asleep, but seeing a

48

light under her door I looked in and was horrified to find her in all her wrinkled nakedness cavorting with a boy of twenty!

I can't describe my shock and disgust, nor the deep embarrassment which she compounded by coming downstairs ten minutes later and making supper for the three of us as if nothing had happened. What's troubling me now is that this late-flowering lust might be a first sign of senility. My mother is fifty and has been widowed for fifteen years.

Rosie had replied:

What's troubling you now, I think, is jealousy. Your weekend lucked out and hers was a doosie. She may be fifty and wrinkled but she can still pull a bit of crumpet when she's got you out of the way!

Dearie, her vagina didn't self-destruct the moment you popped out! If your father had lived I'm sure the pair of them would have enjoyed cavorting at regular intervals. Being a widow she's had to make other arrangements.

Whether she's mad about the boy or just enjoying his earnest attention and strong young body, there is nothing in her behaviour to cause you concern. You really must try not to be such a prude. Good luck to them is all I can say; and do you by any chance know if he has a brother?

She was still chuckling when Matt came in. She showed him why. 'Alex says I can't put it in like that.'

He read it and roared with laughter. 'Tell Alex the proprietor says you absolutely have to put it in just like that.'

Rosie raised an eyebrow. 'She'll be cross with you.'

He sighed, dropped a haunch on to her desk. 'No, she'll just look exquisitely pained and murmur, "It's your newspaper, you must do with it as you see fit," and leave me feeling like a worm.' He looked up then, his strong, intelligent face unhappy. 'What's the matter with me, Rosie? All right, I'm short a foot. But I've got money—at least until this place folds. People reckon I have a certain wit and charm; well, my mum does. I don't pick my nose in public and I don't pat her bottom and call her Sweetie; so what's the problem? *Why* doesn't Alex like me?'

Rosie stared at him incredulously. 'Is that what you think—that she doesn't like you? Dear God,' she groaned, 'they gave a gun and a tank and a platoon of soldiers to a man with all the clear-eyed perceptiveness of a mole-rat. Of course she likes you, you fool of a boy. If she didn't she wouldn't have to work so hard at keeping that small professional distance between you.

'Alex is a woman with a highly developed moral sense, clear on what she expects of others, rigorous in what she demands of herself. She doesn't take advantage of people. Working with somebody like her, any red-blooded male would start foaming at the mouth. Don't think you're the first colleague who's thought he was in love with her.'

Matt tried to challenge that 'thought' but Rosie kept going, as easily diverted as a steamroller. 'How long have you known each other—six months? If she was almost anyone else being pursued by her employer, and he was young and handsome and wealthy—unless this place folds—she'd have had you bedded and wedded long before now. But then, if she'd been anyone but Alex she wouldn't have waited for *you*—she'd have married someone else years ago. The assistant chief administrator at the hospital would have left his wife and three children for Alex.

'And it's not what she wants—not with a secondhand hospital administrator, not with anyone. She doesn't want a man who's bowled over by her beauty. He might think it's the real thing, but infatuation is no foundation for a lasting marriage which is the only sort Alex is interested in. Since she doesn't fool around she isn't going to date anyone who feels like that.'

'Then who the hell is she going to marry?' demanded Matt. 'A blind man? An Eskimo who thinks she isn't fat enough to be beautiful?

51

Who?'

'Matt, Matt,' sighed Rosie, 'put your mouth on hold and give your ears a chance. With any luck, she's going to marry you. You want it, I want it, she wants it.' It didn't strike her there was anything incongruous about the order of that. 'But you have to do it her way. Convince her that you're serious.'

'What?' he said faintly—he'd been trying to get a date and Rosie had all but booked the church and hired the organist, 'Stop singing "The Quartermaster's Stores"?'

It was, thought Rosie, possibly the only chance she'd get to put the landlord of The Spotted Ferret in her debt. But the price was too high. The sight of Matt Gosling, merry on champagne, perched atop the bar and starting the fifteenth verse about the contents of said repository and the unusual purposes to which they might be put was her abiding memory of the night they launched *The Primrose Path*.

'That's not quite what I meant. Suppose you thought every woman you met was after your money. What would a girl have to do to convince you she was different?'

He thought. 'I suppose, if everything she liked doing didn't involve spending a packet.'

'Exactly. So you need to show Alex that you value her for more than her looks. Use her brain: she has a good one. Consult her, ask for her help—not only with work. If you want to make some changes to your flat she'll be happy to offer suggestions as long as you don't give the impression you're changing it for her. Then you can thank her with a meal out—nothing too fancy. She likes Indonesian. It won't happen overnight, but if it's what you both want there has to be a way.'

'*Is* it what she wants? You sound pretty sure but I've seen precious little sign of it.'

'She doesn't know it herself yet. But yes, I'm sure. I've known Alex Fisher for years. You're right for her. Trust me: don't give up.'

'Don't give up, trust you, ask her opinions: got it.' Matt winked and climbed down from the desk as Alex returned.

With one cool glance Alex took in the papers on the desk between them, knew what they'd been discussing, guessed they'd been laughing together. They enjoyed an easy relationship that Alex rather envied, more a friendship than an employer/employee thing, even an amiable one. She sniffed loftily. 'I suppose you agree with Rosie that there's nothing wrong with it.'

Rosie's advice still fresh in his ears, Matt tried to simulate uncertainty, though it sat unconvincingly on his big frank open face. 'Gee, Alex, I don't know—what do you think?'

Alex glared at him and Rosie winced.

*   *   *

The next day, which was a Tuesday, Fee Morris phoned. 'I'm sorry to have put you to so much trouble for nothing. I got a card from Philip this morning. He's fine. He's on Shetland watching a colony of black ducks. Someone was supposed to take over from him after a month but they dropped out and Philip stayed on. He asked me to tell his office he'll be back soon.'

Rosie felt her eyebrows climbing. 'Will they wear that?'

'Oh yes,' said Fee complacently, 'he's always owed leave. They were only worried because he was expected back by the middle of June and now it's August.'

'Did he say why he hadn't written before?'

'Maybe he did and a sheep really did eat the mail. Anyway, everything's fine, I just over-reacted. Thanks for everything.'

'Don't mention it,' said Rosie breezily. 'I'm only sorry I was wrong about the twins.'

She drove out to Foxford to tell Prufrock that the services of his bird-watching connections were no longer needed. She could have phoned but then she'd have missed the chance of casually bumping into the gardener. She made sure of arriving an hour earlier this time, hoping Prufrock's back garden was big enough to require tending for more than half a morning a week.

In one sense she was already too late. Prufrock had spent hours on the phone and tracked down the society for which Philip Morris had gone to Shetland. 'The British Trust for Wildlife—but they're not as big a

54

concern as they sound. They monitor breeding activity in the Scottish islands.'

Rosie failed to contain an unladylike guffaw. 'Do it differently on the Scottish islands, do they? I expect they're at it like rabbits all through the long winter nights, and use the long summer days to catch up on their knitting.'

Prufrock gave a weary sigh. He'd spent his working life amid schoolboy humour, thought he'd left it behind. 'The birds,' he said distinctly, 'not the islanders. They're a bit disorganized, BTW. The first time I called, their Mr Jamison had no record of Philip at all; but I wasn't that impressed with his efficiency so I tried again later and by then he'd found him. He had him down as Maurice Phillips.'

Through the window, ajar to catch the breeze and the scent of flowers, came the sound of hedge-clippers. Rosie affected hardly to notice. 'Shad busy, then?'

Prufrock wasn't deceived for a moment. 'You're interested in topiary, aren't you?'

She stared. 'Am I?'

'Yes,' he said firmly. 'Come and look at mine.'

As topiary goes it was not impressive: a row of vague animal shapes along the back hedge that Prufrock had acquired with the cottage and felt a mild obligation to maintain. They didn't seem to give the gardener much pleasure either: he trimmed their curves with concentration but little enthusiasm.

Sensing Prufrock behind him, without looking round he said, 'One word and I'll whip these buggers off by the feet. You can have serpentines, crenellations, anything.' The gruff voice was more plaintive than hopeful.

'We agreed', Prufrock said patiently, 'that the buggers could stay. And we agreed to refer to them as beasties when we had company.'

That made him turn—so quickly he wobbled on top of the step-ladder. A decent psychic, thought Rosie, would have known she was there all along. 'Hello again.'

It was her first chance to assess more than his brusque departing back and she took it. The basic framework was much as she'd noted out in the lane: age about twenty-five, not tall but strongly built, the curly black hair, heavy brows and olive skin of his mother's kind. But with time to look she absorbed more of the detail.

The heavy brows shaded deep-set dark brown eyes with lashes as long and thick as a girl's. Rosie looked for something different in them—a clarity, perhaps, or else a misty soft focus for seeing things not on general display. Instead she met wariness bordering on suspicion. As if his perception didn't extend so much as confuse his normal faculties; as if he couldn't trust his eyes because of the double-image that sometimes danced before them.

Under her scrutiny a dark flush crept up his cheeks and he jumped down from the steps, holding the hedge-trimmer before him like a weapon. But he wasn't threatening her so much as fending her off. He looked, in the second before reality supervened, as if he were afraid of her.

Taken aback, Rosie blinked and the moment passed; and Prufrock said, 'Shad, this is Miss Primrose Holland of the *Skipley Chronicle*; Miss Holland, my gardener Shad Lucas. Miss Holland's interested in the topiary, Shad.'

'No,' he said at once, the voice gravelly, 'she isn't.'

Rosie sighed. 'No, I'm not. You could take the buggers off by the feet for me, too. I'm interested in how a flat tyre can throw a shadow ahead of itself.'

Of all the ways she could have put it, that may have been the only one that would have kept him standing there. He thought he was a freak. He thought anyone who knew would treat him as a freak. He threw a fast, hot glance at Prufrock because his confidence had been betrayed. But the way she put it was enough to stop him stalking out in mortification disguised as rage. The rough voice was uncertain. 'Shadow?'

Rosie shrugged. 'You've had longer to think about it than I have, you tell me. There's a rationale to everything, even the paranormal. If it exists it can be described; if it can be described it can, eventually, be understood.'

That came out of the gloom like a lifebelt to

a drowning man, and he couldn't be sure if it would support him or hit him on the head and finish him off. Hope flickered like marsh-gas over the mistrust in his eyes. 'You work for a paper?'

'That's right,' said Rosie briskly. 'Before that I was a pathologist.'

Whatever he was expecting, it wasn't that. His eyes flared. 'You want to get your hands on my brain, lady, you wait till I'm dead!'

'I always did,' Rosie said imperturbably.

His lip twitched; he bit it. A tic began to thump under his right eye. Rosie watched with interest, Prufrock with a certain trepidation, to see what would happen next.

When Shad Lucas laughed it was like a roadgrader breaking rocks. The release of tension was palpable. After a moment Rosie added an earthy chuckle of her own and Prufrock a restrained school-masterly harrumph.

'OK,' said Shad, laying down his trimmer in a gesture of defeat, 'you want to talk about it we'll talk about it. But don't expect it to make much sense.'

They went inside and Prufrock put the kettle on. They sat at the table; Shad folded his hands in front of him and kept his eyes on them as he talked. 'I don't know much more about it than you do. This isn't something I've mastered and give demos of. It's something that happens to me—like epilepsy. It comes out of nowhere, it

58

makes no sense, it goes away again. An epileptic can roll round a lot of carpets, bite a lot of chair legs, without being any closer to understanding the mechanics of what's happening.'

Rosie was amazed to hear it put so clearly. She had assumed, from the terseness of their earlier exchange, that his communications skills stopped developing at about the level of the football slogan. That didn't surprise her—it was true of a depressingly large number of young men—but she'd thought it was at the root of his frustration. To have something special going on in your head and lack the words to describe it would be like a painter losing his hands.

But Shad could talk about it if he wanted to; so it was his choice to bottle it up until the pressure filled his head like descending too fast in an aeroplane. But whether he wanted to or not, he needed to talk.

'I tried to believe it was just luck. I made some lucky guesses: everybody does. You have: you've sat thinking about someone, the phone's rung and it's been that person. Or you're talking in the pub about someone you haven't seen for ages and they walk in. You say, Fancy that! You say, That's weird. You don't say that's ESP—I must be psychic.'

'But you know really that it goes beyond luck.'

Defeated, he nodded. 'The point comes

59

where it takes a bigger act of faith to believe in that much coincidence than the alternative.'

Prufrock, too, was impressed: not only with Shad, though he'd never heard him talk this rationally on the subject, but with Rosie. This, of course, was her job: not imparting information that anyone could find in the local library but getting people to talk about things that troubled them, to reach into themselves for the answers. It was, in its own way, a talent as rare as Shad's.

'How does it work? Do you hear voices?'

That drew a little snort of laughter from him. 'Not exactly. It's like there's a radio in another room, and without listening you pick up certain things. Then later you know stuff and can't remember where it came from.' He frowned at her. 'Are you getting any of this?'

'I'm getting all of it,' nodded Rosie. 'Don't underestimate yourself: you may not know why this happens but you have a sophisticated appreciation of what's happening. You thought I'd spoken to you, in the lane?'

'For a moment. Then I realized you hadn't and it was—this. But if I'd tried to explain you'd have jumped back in your car, locked the doors and thumped the horn to attract attention. So I got the hell out. It's not something you can discuss with strangers in the street. They'd call a policeman.'

'Is that what you're afraid of? Losing control of your life?'

60

He jerked as if she'd kicked him under the table. Rosie knew from his face that she'd struck home. 'Maybe.'

'No one can make you do anything you don't want to. This—gift? talent?—of yours is nothing to be afraid of.'

He bridled. 'Don't patronize me. Whatever it is, it's mine. I'll judge whether it's a bane or a blessing.'

Rosie nodded, refusing to argue with him. 'So are your Malpighian pyramids. You want to tell me if they're good news or bad news?'

That made him blink and, after a moment, back down. 'This isn't covered in your textbooks.'

'So write your own. But don't run away from it. It's only paranormal because we don't know enough.' Rosie chuckled. 'Think of it as a sport that's appeared in a pot of hyacinths. Study it. Find out what it does, what it's good for, the conditions that suit it. Try to direct it instead of letting it direct you. If you can get that distant radio to say things like "He's got a pair of aces!" and "Raise him, he's bluffing!" you could be rich.'

She was trying to picture him in evening dress and diamond studs, breaking the bank at Monte Carlo. Shad was thinking in terms of a new Land Rover.

'I don't want to be rich. I want—' He tailed off in silence.

Rosie prompted him gently. 'You want to be
61

rid of it?'

'No, not that either.' The effort of confronting it furrowed his brow. He shrugged awkwardly. 'What you said, I suppose. To be in control.'

'It may be,' suggested Rosie, 'that the best way to do that is to make a point of using it.'

His gaze sharpened. 'I am not wearing an earring and joining my mother on Southend Pier!'

The image was engaging; Rosie let it go only reluctantly. 'That isn't quite what I had in mind. A lot of people come to me for help. Pretty often it's stuff I have some competence in—medicine, or relationships, or how to get rid of noisy neighbours—pretty often I can tell them something useful.

'But sometimes I can't begin to help, and neither could anyone I could recommend. Problems like—hell, I don't know. Missing persons. People's kids have run off to London and they don't know if they're alive or dead. The police have given up and they don't know where to turn. Maybe instead of telling me the time of the next bus you could tell them to go to Camden Lock or wherever. Do you think?'

She expected a yes, or a no, or a maybe. She didn't expect him to recoil and look away so fast she'd barely time to register the anguish in his eyes; or that Prufrock would flinch, and reach for the young man's shoulder, change his mind halfway and clasp his hands together so

62

tightly the knuckles whitened.

She knew she'd said the wrong thing. She didn't know how. 'What? *What?* Tell me, somebody!'

After a moment Shad mumbled, 'Tell her,' and Prufrock did.

CHAPTER FIVE

Matt Gosling spent the afternoon with the accountants. There was good news and bad news.

The good news was that the *Skipley Chronicle* was operating at a profit for the first time in twenty years. The bad news was that there was twenty years' worth of neglect to the building to be made good which would swallow up any foreseeable surplus for most of the foreseeable future.

'Can we prioritize?' he suggested. 'Do what has to be done now and the rest when our finances can stand it?'

The accountants gave a discreet cough. They tended to act in unison, like choral speakers, as if there were safety in numbers. 'Actually, we've already done that. These *are* the things that have to be done now.'

'What are we talking of—a bank loan?' He'd managed thus far on family money. When he started this the *Chronicle* would not have seemed a sound investment to a bank whereas the Goslings, and his mother's family the Fanes, ran to tribes of wealthy widows and spinsters all anxious to help the poor wounded soldier. It was a sentiment Matt exploited shamelessly in the hectic weeks he was putting the deal together but he'd been looking forward to paying a dividend on their investment. There would be less pleasure in telling them their profits had fixed the roof to the satisfaction of the Health & Safety Executive.

The accountants looked embarrassed. 'A bank would tell you to knock the building down and start afresh.'

Matt had been told that before. Even if he could have afforded to he didn't want to. There was history in every grimy brick here, he wasn't swapping the defunct gas-lamps and the printer's ghost for a glass and concrete box on the ring road. 'Well, I'm not going back to the aged aunts.'

'Then you'll need to reinvest all profits for the next five years and most of them for the five years after that. Or—'

'Or you could trim the outgoings. Use less newsprint—two fewer pages per issue would give you a buffer against emergencies. And while you aren't exactly overstaffed, for every post you can lose by natural wastage you're immediately fifteen to twenty thousand pounds a year better off.'

Matt breathed hard at them. 'We're a

newspaper. You want me to cut the people who write it and the paper we print it on? Hey, maybe we should stop buying ink—nobody'd notice that little economy either.'

Accountants have no sense of humour: it's required for their final exams. They sniffed censoriously. 'You're paying for our advice, Mr Gosling, and this is it. You're fortunate to have access to private money. If your family will continue to support you, the facts of commercial life need never trouble you. But if you wish the *Chronicle* to succeed as a business you must learn to make difficult decisions. If you want the newspaper on a proper financial footing the readers have to pay you more than it costs to produce not less. You can increase the price; but if you put it up ten per cent and ten per cent of readers stop buying it you've gained nothing but ill-will. Or you can cut costs. We've pointed out two places where costs can be trimmed relatively painlessly. It's entirely up to you whether you take that advice.'

When they'd gone Matt sat alone in his top-floor office and pondered. But the accountants were right: the bottom line was, he had to meet the bills. He reflected bitterly that being able to abseil out of a helicopter was no help in running a shaky business.

About five thirty it struck him he was achieving nothing and might as well worry at home. As he opened his door he all but ran into Alex's fist, raised for a diffident tap.

'Were you looking for me?' It was a stupid thing to say: no one else used this floor.

But Alex was so relieved to have found him she didn't notice. She looked uncharacteristically flustered, a sweet disorder that kindled in Matt the sort of feelings he had previously only had for the regimental silver.

Her eyes were troubled. 'Thank heavens I caught you. If you'd left I don't know what I'd have done.'

If Matt could have put one sentence in her mouth, that was it. But she wasn't a helpless girl, she was an intelligent woman of nearly thirty who'd spent years sorting out little local difficulties. At the hospital she averted bloody war when the chief physician's new office was built over the chief surgeon's parking space. Matt couldn't imagine what disaster had led her to beg his help with those eyes.

'Whatever's the matter?' The germ of a suspicion seeded. 'Is it Rosie?'

Alex ushered him to the lift, punched for the second floor. 'I didn't know what to do. She's too big to smuggle out unnoticed, and Dan'll sack her if he finds out.'

'Dan wouldn't dare sack Rosie!' exclaimed Matt delightedly. But Alex couldn't share his amusement and the laughter died in his eyes. His brow creased. 'Alex, tell me what's happened. Where is Rosie?'

Alex dipped her gaze in deep

66

embarrassment. 'She's in her office. Matt—she's drunk.'

So it wasn't a tragedy after all. Matt began to grin again. 'One too many down The Spotted Ferret? Oh, Alex, this is a newspaper—tiddly journos are part of the ambience.'

Alex refused to be reassured. 'She's not tiddly, she's drunk—too drunk to walk. I don't know how to get her home. I can't carry her.'

Matt baulked from saying he could. Though one of her greatest admirers, he recognized that manoeuvring Rosie, dead drunk, through the narrow corridors, in and out of the dumb-waiter lift and down the front steps would be a challenge worthy of the Royal Tournament. 'We'll manage together.'

Alex hadn't exaggerated. Rosie hadn't had one over the odds. She wasn't tiddly, merry or well oiled; or tired and emotional, the worse for wear or three sheets to the wind. She was drunk. She lay over the desk, head cradled in her arms, snoring. From the litter of papers on the floor this may have happened fairly abruptly. A whisky bottle lay on its side in her in-tray. The glass had rolled off the desk into the waste-paper basket.

'Rosie?' Matt shook her shoulder gently, then more insistently. 'Rosie!' All the reply he got was a mumbled 'Bugger off.'

'We'll take the back stairs,' Matt decided. 'I'll get hold of a van. If we shovel her in the back no one'll see the state she's in.'

67

'Can you do that?' asked Alex, her eyes hopeful. 'Borrow a van?'

'I don't have to borrow it,' said Matt. 'I *own* it.'

Which would have made no difference at all if Rosie had got drunk a day later. Wednesday was when the *Chronicle* moved into top gear. The paper was dated Thursday so the pages were set up and shipped to the printer's on Wednesday. From early morning the blanks were on the stone, being pasted with strips of news and photographs; as each was finished it was taken by van to the printers where it was turned into an etched plate. By then a van should have arrived with the next page. An hour after the last one, the front page, arrived the plates were clamped into the press. Printing started at six o'clock on Thursday morning and the first papers were on their way to the newsagents an hour after that. On Wednesday the vans were in constant use.

On the other hand, with the building bedlam all day, a fat woman waving a whisky bottle and singing the post-watershed verses of 'The Quartermaster's Stores' might have been hustled through reception without anyone noticing.

But this was Tuesday so the building was emptying from five o'clock onwards: first the girls who ran the office and took the ads; then the reporters, dribbling out—mostly towards The Spotted Ferret—as they finished their stories; then chief photographer Jonah McLeod who wanted a clear deck for the last-minute pictures he would barely have time to develop before going to press but which would be stale news by next week.

That still didn't leave the building empty. Some of the setters would stay till about eight—there'd be too much to do tomorrow to leave anything that could be done today—and Dan Sale would be in his office later than that. Every week he worried that he'd overlooked something, that he'd end up with stories with no photos or photos with no captions, that he'd forgotten to allocate someone to the magistrate's court or he'd promised something to someone and given it no thought since. Tuesday evenings he stayed late in the office, not so much doing things as fretting over them.

Alex was right about one thing: if Dan had known he had a rat-arsed agony aunt on the premises he wouldn't have stopped at worrying. He was an experienced and pragmatic journalist who didn't expect the earth in return for a week's wage, but some things he insisted on. One was being fit to do the job all the time you were on duty. Anyone who'd drunk too much to drive was sent home to think of a good reason why they should keep their job. Someone who'd drunk too much to walk was unlikely to come up with a reason good enough.

The back stairs were all but deserted by six

o'clock. They might have run into a setter sneaking out for a fag—they were supposed to use their breaks for that but it was more important to keep ash out of the computers than it was to keep the keyboards humming every minute—but that wouldn't be a problem to Matt. There wasn't much scope to blackmail the proprietor.

But it was hard work hauling Rosie to her feet and steering her down four flights of stone steps, particularly since Alex, who had no trouble with stairs, wasn't strong enough to hold her and Matt, who was, had. But they managed somehow and Matt left the women on the back step while he went for a van. Alex had a chic little run-about that Rosie had trouble getting into even when she was sober; Matt drove a middle-aged Porsche. They could have poured her into the Korean tank but someone would notice if either of them drove with Rosie lolling against the other in the back seat. The advantage of a van, apart from the low loading platform, was the solid sides.

After an anxious five minutes, not improved by Rosie's suddenly becoming garrulous and wanting to explain her behaviour in maudlin detail, Alex heard the engine and the blue and green van backed round the corner and up to the steps. 'Seen anyone?'

Alex shook her head. 'So far, so good.' Then she gave a little, faintly hysterical giggle. 'It's like sneaking back into school after lights out,

70

only in reverse.'

Matt was enchanted. 'You were at boarding school?'

'I was at a *convent* school, my dear, the *only* way to produce young ladies.' She edged Rosie towards the open doors.

'Some young lady you were, sneaking back after lights out! Where did you go to?' Matt hefted Rosie into the back of the van as if she'd been a sack of last week's returns.

Alex flicked him a smile. 'We used to slip away to the monthly hop at the Anglican church hall, and hope to God the nuns never found out.'

'And did they?'

'I think they may have suspected. One night when we got back we found a cow had been scratching on the side gate and it wouldn't open. So someone had left a step-ladder where we could climb over the wall.'

At the vicarage Matt reversed the van up to the front door and they trundled Rosie into the hall like fourteen stone of potatoes. Alex looked doubtfully at the staircase. 'Do we put her to bed?'

'She can sleep it off on the sofa,' decided Matt. 'We've taken enough risks for one day. I'd just as soon not rupture myself as well.'

He wouldn't have conspired against his editor for just anyone. But Rosie was worth it; and for Alex he'd have risked the rupture as well. When she suggested tea he didn't hurry

71

off. They ate in the kitchen, with Rosie snoring on the sitting-room sofa.

'What happened—do you know?' Matt knew Rosie was a woman of appetite rather than abstinence. He'd seen her merry before but he hadn't seen her drunk, and he was frankly dismayed. He wasn't a prude about alcohol—to most soldiers TT means the motorcycle races on the Isle of Man—but whatever he'd told Alex, drinking at work was the shortest way on to the dole. Rosie Holland was enough of a loose cannon sober.

'I've no idea. I've never seen her like this before. She was already well away when she got back mid-afternoon, and she had a bottle with her and kept drinking till she passed out.'

'And she didn't say why?'

'She mumbled something about missing persons. I couldn't make head nor tail of it. Um.' Her eyes made a wordless appeal. 'Will you tell Dan?'

Matt had already asked himself that. 'No. But I won't lie to him either. If he gets wind of it and asks, I'll tell him what happened.'

'He'll sack her.'

'Possibly. I'll try to talk him out of it but it's his decision.'

Alex nodded acceptance. Then she smiled. 'I don't know why I came to the *Chronicle*. It was a crazy thing to do. But I'd be sorry to leave now, like this.'

Matt frowned. 'You're not Siamese twins,

you know. And you're not responsible for Rosie's indiscretions. If Rosie leaves there'll be another women's page editor.'

'Yes, of course. All the same, I can't imagine doing this with anyone else.' Suddenly she looked anxious. 'I'm sorry, Matt, that sounded like a threat and I didn't mean it to. I just think I might look for something easier on the nerves.'

'Being PA to another women's page editor *would* be easier on the nerves.'

Alex chuckled and didn't deny it, but Matt knew that she wouldn't stay if Rosie left. And he didn't see what, in honour, he could do about it.

By the time they'd washed the dishes there were signs of life from the sofa. Possibly not intelligent life; possibly a life-form developed on a swamp planet, where the ability to hump around and moan represented a pinnacle of evolution, but life nonetheless. Alex sighed and made some more coffee.

By the time Rosie had showered and changed her clothes, and had enough black coffee to antifoul a barge, she was capable of appreciating what she'd done. She blew her cheeks out apologetically. 'Matt, what can I say?'

'How about, It won't happen again.'

'It won't happen again,' she echoed obediently. She put tender fingertips to her skull. 'Dear God, I've *seen* brains like this!

Whatever must my liver look like?'

'Rosie, why?' Alex sounded terribly disappointed.

Rosie sighed and, very gently, shook her head. 'That boy. That poor bloody boy.'

Neither of them knew what she was talking about. Matt said, 'What boy?'

'The one I told you about. The gardener? The one who knew about my puncture before it happened.'

'What about him?'

Rosie ground the heels of her hands into her eyes. 'I asked if he'd help me look for missing persons!'

'So?'

*   *   *

Dark head bowed Shad Lucas mumbled, 'Tell her,' and Prufrock did. He stood by the kitchen window, watching the sunny garden through the glazing bars, and began to talk in a voice at once precise and gentle.

'Shad's mother may be the least gifted clairvoyant in the business but his uncle was an expert diviner. He dowsed for water, for underground pipes and cables, and for minerals. He could dowse on the ground and off maps. At the peak of his powers Jacob Appleby travelled all over the British Isles to advise mining and construction companies and farms.

'Shad was barely into his teens when Jacob taught him to dowse, but he had the gift, too. If Jacob had lived another year they were going into business together. Then Jacob died, and multimillion pound enterprises declined to dig expensive holes on the word of a sixteen-year-old, and that was that.'

The old man glanced at his gardener then. Shad didn't look up but he said, 'Keep going,' his voice lower than ever.

Prufrock turned to Rosie. 'You haven't lived here very long so if someone mentions the Clee Hills you probably think of an open stretch of uplands covered with bracken, sheep and ponies; a nice spot for a family picnic. But for most of 1988 and '89, nobody took their family to the Clee Hills.

'The first child disappeared from a caravan with her parents sleeping a few feet away. She was three; someone stole her through an open window. Police and volunteers combed the hills for eight days and found nothing. Within a month another child was missing.

'In the end there were seven, all under ten. The first three were on holiday, but after that there were no tourists and the children were from local farms and villages. Panic spread from Birmingham to the Welsh Marches. People moved their families out of the area. Those who couldn't leave watched their children constantly; but one little boy vanished from the cab of his father's tractor in the time

75

it took him to open a gate.

'The police set up a task-force to find the person responsible. In the summer of 1989 they arrested a Kidderminster man whose work for an animal transport firm regularly took him into the Ludlow area. Tony Collier was questioned after a workmate saw a child's comic in his cab. Collier said he'd given a woman a lift when her car broke down, her child must have left it behind. But the police didn't believe him and extensive enquiries failed to find the woman concerned.

'The task force believed they had the abductor,' said Prufrock. 'He was certainly in the area on two occasions when children went missing, and couldn't show he was anywhere else at any of the other times. He was an odd, uncommunicative man without family or friends. If there's such a thing as a typical child molester, Collier was it.

'But there was no proof. The comic could have come from anywhere. Collier denied everything and nothing more was found in the lorry or at his home. The police desperately needed either a body or items that could be identified as belonging to a missing child. But there are seventy square miles of not very much in the Clee Hills: how do you set about finding a few tiny graves?

'You may be aware,' Prufrock said quietly, 'that sometimes, as a last resort, the police consult psychics. If it's only a one-in-a-thousand chance it's worth taking when there's nothing else. One of the officers knew of a dowser with a good reputation. Jacob Appleby was no longer available, but his apprentice was.'

Though Rosie would have said her job involved more listening than talking, in fact she could rarely resist interrupting if a tale took more than three sentences to tell. All that had kept her silent this long was a sense of deep foreboding. 'Shad went dowsing for dead babies?' Shock quivered in her voice. 'Dear God, he wasn't much more than a child himself! Whatever were the police thinking of?'

'They were thinking', said Shad, biting the words off one at a time to keep them under control, 'of putting a deeply dangerous man where he couldn't kill again. They couldn't hold him without evidence: they'd have had to let him go, knowing he'd immediately go looking for another kid. They asked me to help and I said I'd try. What else could I say?'

'Nothing,' agreed Rosie softly. But she could imagine what it must have been like for a sensitive teenager trying to tune in not to the murmur of subsurface water or the buzz of a power-cable but to the terror and desolation of an abducted child in the hands of its murderer. Having been asked there was indeed nothing else he could do; but she wondered how those who asked him managed to sleep at night. 'Did you—succeed?' She didn't know how else to put it.

'Yes.'

'You found—what? Clothes, belongings?' She swallowed. 'A body?'

'I found three bodies,' he said dully. 'Two little girls and a boy. He'd buried them in old badger setts. When forensics found fibres from his clothes on theirs he confessed and took the police to the other four.'

The slow seconds stretched into minutes, the silence falling about them like ash. It seemed impossible to follow those words with any others. Prufrock stayed by the kitchen window. Shad sat at the table, eyes nailed to the earth-grimed hands knotted in front of him. Rosie was rooted to her chair, could not have moved to save her soul. She didn't know what to say to him.

After a long time, forcing her voice level, she said, 'You know, of course, that you didn't just find dead children—didn't just give their parents a proper chance to mourn. You saved the lives of God knows how many others he'd have killed before he could have been caught any other way.'

Shad nodded jerkily. 'I know.'

'But you haven't done it since.'

'No.'

'And then some smart cow comes along and wonders if you've ever thought of using your gift to look for missing persons. Shad, I'm

78

sorry.'

He looked at her then and a little fugitive smile stole across his face. 'It's all right. It was a long time ago.'

Rosie shook her head and her voice was hollow with disbelief. 'Something like that? It was yesterday.'

Shad closed his eyes. He said simply, 'Yes.' Then quietly he began to cry.

*   *   *

She told Matt and Alex everything, up to that point. She told them about the murdered children, how they had been found and what it had cost.

But she didn't tell them that a young man of twenty-five, gypsy eyes haunted by an eight-year-old memory of the feeling of evil, had sat bowed over his knotted hands and cried like a lost child himself; or that she, stirred by some instinct she didn't even know she had, flowed round the table like water and gathered him into her arms and cried with him, the great salt drops running off her nose, while he spent his misery on her breast.

CHAPTER SIX

In a normal week the feature pages, including *The Primrose Path*, were set up on the Monday, clearing the stone for news stories. By Tuesday Rosie was already working on next week's page and so largely missed the *Chronicle*'s big push every Wednesday. Her main concern was to watch for last-minute developments demanding changes to something she'd written as much as a week earlier. She dreaded a man appearing in Wednesday's court, and thus Thursday's paper, for putting his wife in hospital when that week's *Path* was advising her to tackle him about their problems face to face in the confidence that he'd respond reasonably and creatively.

Underneath her the building buzzed. From eight in the morning until late at night there would be no such thing as a formal break: people would grab cigarettes, meals and even inspections of the plumbing as and when the job could spare them. It was fourteen hours of mayhem but it was also what the previous six days had all been about so people threw themselves into the fray with energy and purpose. At close of play there was a little weekly ceremony where Dan shut the last page into the back of the van and sent it off to the printers with the blessing: 'Another bloody miracle.'

So while the reporting and printing staff started sharp at eight on Wednesdays, Rosie tended to meander in at about nine thirty by which time Alex had the post sorted. The first letter she read set the expletives Alex would

80

later delete whirling in her head.

I like fried rice as much as the next person, but how many Chinese restaurants and laundries and trinket-shops does any one town need?

I come from Glasgow, and though my husband and I have lived in Skipley for many years we still visit friends and family in Scotland. We're just back from a fortnight with my sister in Strathclyde, and I was amazed at how things have changed in the last year. The place is awash with Chinese immigrants.

Not that I have anything against them— they seem nice enough people, hard-working and respectable, the children always polite and well turned out. But why so many? The Home Office must know it's the numbers that make people resentful. Can't they direct new immigrants to towns that need their services rather than those that already have spring rolls and paper fans coming out of their ears?

The short answer,

Rosie wrote when she'd finished spitting tacks,

is no. This country has rigorous immigration controls—if we hadn't been born here they'd never have let you and me in—and anyone

81

who meets them is entitled to settle anywhere he chooses. The Chinese you speak of might well seem hard-working, respectable and polite: they wouldn't have been admitted otherwise.

What exactly is your problem? There are parts of the UK where people live in fear of insult, robbery, assault and worse from neighbourhood children: are you really this worried about the colour of their skin? I think you need to get out more, see a bit of the real world. I know places in England where your accent will be enough to make you unwelcome, where they feel the Scots are all very well in their place but that place is Scotland and if they see another Fair Isle sweater they'll scream.

But then you'd write to me again, wouldn't you? 'Why are the English so *intolerant ...?*'

She was still fuming when the phone rang and it was Fiona Morris again. Now she sounded frightened. 'I don't know what the hell's going on but something is; and if it doesn't mean Philip's in trouble I don't know what else.'

'Fiona—Fee—calm down,' Rosie said sternly. 'Calm down and tell me what's happened.'

'I got a postcard. From Philip.'

Rosie frowned. 'I know that. You told me that yesterday.'

'No, not that one. Another one. Oh, God,'

she moaned then, 'I can't explain over the phone. Can I meet you—can we talk?'

Rosie wrestled with her conscience, but not for long. Squinted at sideways, in certain lights, an early lunch with Fee Morris almost looked like work. She could convince Matt, even Dan; but Alex would look at her as if she'd had her hand in the till. Alex hadn't yet forgiven her for getting drunk.

'Yes, of course. But it'll be a madhouse here all day. Can we meet for lunch? Where are you?'

'I'm at school. I'm taking a summer scheme. I can get away about twelve.'

Fee's school was no distance from Rosie's vicarage. 'Do you know the Palmyra Café, behind the cinema? I'll see you there at ten past twelve. And try not to worry. Whatever it is, there'll be a rational explanation.'

'Yes?' Fee's voice posed an edgy challenge. 'Well, I can't wait to hear it.'

The traffic was heavy and by the time Rosie was parking her car Fiona Morris had found a table. She looked frail, her skin bleached by the nagging worry.

No one ever accused Rosie of lacking colour. She arrived in the Palmyra Café like a Silk Route caravan descending on a desert town, all noise and bustle and blithe disorder, so that people watched in amazement and wondered what manner of creature she was; and, a little later, why her mere presence made their own lives seem drab by comparison.

Except for the proprietor, who'd grown used to her in the last six months. 'Coffee, Rosie?'

'In a bucket,' she said fervently. 'And sandwiches—lots of sandwiches.' Hip first she threaded the inadequate space between table and chair.

Fee delved into the satchel she used as a handbag, put the two cards on the table. 'There. Give me a rational explanation for those.'

One was a bad picture of Edinburgh Castle with the stamp askew, dated the first of June but post-marked the first week in August. In black biro a sprawling hand had written 'Fee, Change of plan. Edinburgh too hot for comfort. Can I crash on your couch a few days? I'll explain when I see you. Sorry to dump on you like this. Love, Phi.'

'Phi?' asked Rosie, deadpan.

The younger woman shrugged. 'Fee, Phi—a sort of nursery joke we never quite outgrew.'

Rosie picked up the second card. It was a better picture of a less hackneyed scene: a great stone tower, half tumbled but still massive, looming against heather hills and a wine-dark sea. The caption read 'The Broch of Mousa, Shetland.' The postmark was Lerwick, also the previous week.

This time the sprawling letters were in blue ink. 'Fee, My relief never showed up so I'm still with the Scoters. Call my office, will you, make

84

my apologies? Should be back before long. Weather a bit mixed but the birds are fine and so am I. Look after yourself. Love, Phi.

Fee was drumming the table-top with a fore-finger. 'It makes no sense, Rosie. First he writes he's on his way here; then he doesn't post the card for a couple of months; then he does post it, in Edinburgh, and immediately takes off for Shetland and writes again as if he'd been there for weeks. What the hell's going on?'

'It is odd,' Rosie admitted. 'I suppose they're both Philip's handwriting?'

Fee nodded. 'I'd know it anywhere. I teach infants to write: I'd strangle any who couldn't do better than that.'

'And the one from Shetland arrived yesterday, and the one from Edinburgh, that he wrote two months ago, arrived this morning?' Rosie studied it. 'He put a first-class stamp on it; he needed it to reach you quickly, he wanted you to put him up the next night.' She frowned. 'But as soon as he'd written it he changed his mind and didn't post it. Two months later it was posted, in Edinburgh. How come, if he's on Shetland?'

'He lives in Edinburgh. He has a room behind the Royal Mile. But he hasn't been there since the first of June. I checked with his landlady.'

'A room?'

Fee flicked a wan smile. 'Not much to show
85

for your life when you're a thirty-two-year-old professional, is it? But Philip never put much store in possessions. He's more interested in doing things: a house, even a flat, would have tied him down. He just wanted somewhere to stay between projects. His landlady treats him as one of her family.'

'When did you speak to her?'

'Before I wrote to you, when I started getting anxious. She said he'd come home for one day then left again.'

'Maybe you should call her back. Maybe she's heard from him by now. We're only five minutes from my house. We'll call from there.' Rosie looked round. 'Gerry, you couldn't bag these sandwiches for me?'

Quite apart from the fact that a prudent café owner takes care of a regular with a hearty appetite, Gerry Fish would have done anything Rosie asked. He thought she was wonderful. 'Do you want a doggy thermos, too?'

Rosie laughed. 'No, I'll make some fresh when we get there. Actually'—she looked ruefully at the coffee pot—'I seem to have drunk most of it anyway.'

Fee was on foot so they took the Korean tank. As Rosie pulled into her drive she found it already occupied, by a Land Rover painted like a patchwork quilt.

Fee said, 'If I'm going to be in the way—'

'No,' said Rosie, 'it's just a friend of mine— well, a friend's gardener; I suppose a client in a way . . .' She abandoned the attempt to explain. 'Come and meet him.'

Shad had given up waiting for the door to be answered and left his offering in a bucket in the porch. He'd come at midday precisely because she would probably be out. He'd been embarrassed about seeing her again. But some imperfectly understood sense of owing her something had sent him anyway, armed with enough flowers to fill the house.

She didn't recognize half of them. He'd made no attempt to sort them: they jostled like commuters on a train, shoulder to shoulder in not enough space, their colours arguing. They were a gardener's bouquet rather than a florist's, thought Rosie, selected more for fecundity than charm, gathered not one by one but by the armful. He'd picked them at speed because if he didn't get this done quickly he wouldn't do it at all.

Inside the porch, preoccupied with the flowers, he hadn't heard the car. The first he knew that Rosie was home was when he turned on the step and practically walked into her. A flush raced up into his cheeks and he shoved his hands into the pockets of his jeans as if she'd caught him stealing. He mumbled, 'I brought some flowers. I . . . yesterday . . . I wanted—' He ground to an awkward, toe-curled halt.

Rosie smiled. 'They're beautiful. You grew them?'

It was a pretty stupid thing to ask a gardener. For a moment Shad looked taken aback, then he gave his gruff laugh. 'Yeah. But I bought the bucket.'

Rosie laughed, too. 'I'll treasure it.' Behind her Fee was growing restless. 'Sorry—Fee Morris, Shad Lucas. Fee, that other bird-watcher I told you about? Shad works for him.'

Fee had been about to hurry Rosie inside so they could call Mrs Mackey. That stopped her: they might need the bird-watcher again. She nodded a minimalist greeting.

An awful temptation stirred in Rosie's breast. She tried to dismiss it. She waved the carrier bag from the Palmyra Café. 'I've got a ton of sandwiches and I'm going to make some coffee. You'll stay for lunch, Shad?'

He hadn't wanted to come so much as felt he should. He'd been glad when no one answered the door, was happy to leave the flowers in the porch with a note scribbled on the back of a seed packet. Now he was glad he'd seen Rosie and thanked her in person; but he would still have pleaded an urgent appointment and left if it hadn't been for the girl with her hart's eyes and her straight slender limbs and aura of mingled strength and vulnerability. A girl like a willow, delicate and enduring. Her watchful silence spoke to him. 'OK. Thanks.'

Rosie hadn't a psychic bone in her body—she knew because of all the three-legged racehorses that had stumbled home for her—

but she could see what would happen next, why the offer of a tuna salad sandwich was keeping him here when all his instincts were to return to the safety of his gardens. Why he was talking to her but looking past her shoulder. Shad Lucas and Fee Morris? At least they'd never be bored.

While Rosie was making the coffee Fee phoned Mrs Mackey in Edinburgh. The ringing went on almost long enough for her to give up before the landlady answered breathlessly. She'd been vacuuming the top floor.

She remembered Fee from their earlier conversation. 'And how is Philip? Any new birds to report?'

'That's what I'm calling about. I'm still not sure where he is. I don't suppose you've heard from him?'

'Me? No. Not so much as a postcard. But these places he goes, they're pretty wild, aren't they?'

'Well, yes,' admitted Fee. 'Still, he's always managed to write before. And in fact I have had postcards from him—two since the weekend. Trouble is, they put him in two different places.'

'Ah.' That meant something to Mrs Mackey. 'Was one of them from here? A poorish picture of Edinburgh Castle?'

Fee stared at the phone. 'How do you know that?'

'I posted it,' explained the landlady. 'On

Monday. My son was helping me clean Philip's room. He was looking at a book and that fell out. It was stamped and all. I thought he'd forgotten to send it, so I put it in the post. Was that wrong?'

The woman was so obviously anxious that Fee regretted her sharpness. 'I'm glad you did. That explains why it was written in June but only arrived this morning.' But that was all it explained.

Shad was in the garden, weighing up how much work would be needed to reclaim the wasteland it had become. His initial impression was that there was nothing worth saving and the site could be cleared by a bulldozer. Fee took advantage of his absence to tell Rosie what the landlady had said.

Rosie listened in silence. Even when she couldn't think of one she'd felt there must be a rational explanation. The alternative was that a grown man had been kidnapped either while bird-watching or on the InterCity to Birmingham. Now they knew why Fee got that first card two months late but not why it had been written or why, once written, it had not been sent.

'Rosie, what am I going to do? Go to Shetland, start knocking on doors? I'll do it if I can't think of anything better, and maybe I'll find him. But what if I don't? I'm so scared of not finding him, I almost don't want to look.'

Rosie put a coffee pot like a Salvation Army

tea urn on to a tray with three mugs and the plate of sandwiches. 'Fee, we're going to sort this out. I don't know how, but we are. Come on, let's join Shad outside. Er . . . bring the cards.'

The L-shape of the vicarage half enclosed a paved area between the kitchen and drawing-room windows. With its teak table and chairs, and half a dozen terracotta pots planted with herbs and strawberries, it was the extent of Rosie's interest in her garden, and she probably wouldn't have done that much if it hadn't made a perfect place to sit with a drink of an evening, the red brick walls that had spent all day absorbing the sun gently paying it back.

Rosie poured the coffee and dropped into a chair. Shad was almost out of sight in the wreckage of the vegetable plot. She raised her voice. 'Come and get it while it's hot.'

Then she took the postcards from Fee and spread them on the table in front of her, face down, scrutinizing the writing. There were only two possibilities. Either Philip Morris wrote them both, in which case why did he write what he did? Or he only wrote one, in which case who wrote the other, which, and why? The eyes she raised to Fee were hard, her voice flat. 'I'm going to try something. Don't say anything, whatever happens.'

Shad sat down where he could still see the garden. 'It's got possibilities. The bones are good—brick walls, a few good trees, and you've

91

some York stone paths buried under the rubbish. If you want to spend some money on it sometime you could have a decent garden.'

They made an odd gathering, Rosie thought ruefully: a young woman sick with worry about her brother, a young man who talked about shrubs and stone paths and could hear the earth's heartbeat, and the famously wise and witty Primrose Holland reduced to nodding and smiling by repugnance at what she was going to do next.

It was underhand, it was mean—knowing what she did it was inexcusable—but she didn't know what else to do. It was a failing of hers that she would do the wrong thing before she would do nothing. So she steeled herself and did it.

She forced a smile and passed the two postcards to Shad. 'Fee's looking for her brother. Apparently he's on Shetland studying black ducks.'

He took the cards and Rosie waited, holding her breath.

Shad looked cursorily at the pictures, then turned them over to read the captions on the back. He held them out to Fee. 'Who's the other one from?'

Fee frowned. Even without reading the messages he couldn't have missed the distinctive hand scrawled across each of them. 'They're both from Philip. He wrote one before he went, the other after he got there.'

92

There was a sense of time slowing down, of events on the edge of happening, of the path dividing, and one track petering out in 'Oh' and 'Really' and 'I see', and the other . . .

His sturdy hand with the good earth grained into the calluses was already opening to part with them when the awareness of something wrong overtook him and he hesitated, arm outstretched, a kind of hiatus in his face as if the next message, the one that said 'Lift your thumb', had failed to arrive. Then his heavy brows twitched and gathered, and his eyes flickered round the patio as if for a moment he didn't know where he was. He cleared his throat.

'Oh no he didn't,' he said.

CHAPTER SEVEN

'This matters,' said Rosie quietly, 'so let's get it right. You say those cards were written by different people?'

Concentration drew his brows together and his dark gaze turned inward. For perhaps a minute the women watched Shad's broad, blunt hands spread on the cards and no one spoke.

At the end of that time he looked up, blinking his eyes clear. 'Sure of it.' There was a slight breathiness to his voice as if he'd been exerting himself.

'In spite of the writing? I mean, look at it—how many people who can write at all write as badly as that?'

He moved his hands apart on the table-top, clear of the cards. He didn't look at them again, eyed Rosie steadily. 'I don't know anything about handwriting. Maybe it takes a real expert to copy someone else's writing; or maybe anyone could do it with a bit of practice. I don't know. I know about two things, and one of them is the way things give off energy as distinctive as a signature. That tells me those cards came from two different people.'

He rose abruptly and Rosie thought she'd pushed too hard, that he was going to stalk out and leave her in the debris. But that wasn't it. He was still speaking, with a quiet authority that would have impressed her if she'd known nothing of his history. 'You don't have to believe me. I'm not the Pope, I never claimed to be infallible. I could be wrong. But I don't think so. You wanted my opinion, that's it: if Philip Morris wrote one of those cards, someone else wrote the other.'

If Rosie had sprung this on Shad like an ambush, she'd dropped it on Fee like a thunderbolt. It had taken her almost till now to work out that they were serious, that it wasn't a sick joke. She knew now from the expressions of both of them, from the gravelly intensity of the man's voice. It might be ridiculous but it wasn't a joke. They really were talking about—

what, telepathy?—as if it might offer some clue to Philip's whereabouts.

The muscles of her jaw had seized up in disbelief. She coughed them free. 'Which one did he write?'

Shad looked at her almost in surprise, as if he'd forgotten she was there. He shook his head. 'I don't know. They aren't the same, that's all.'

Rosie bit her lip. 'If one of these cards was forged—because they're certainly meant to look the same—it has to be the one from Shetland. If whatever made Edinburgh too hot for him happened, the second card could have been sent as a cover-up, to stop you getting anxious enough to go looking for him. But I can't think of any motive for forging the first one. To make you think he's in trouble when he isn't? What would be the point?'

Fee was still looking hard at Shad. She didn't know whether she believed him or not. Almost the worst thing about Philip's disappearance was the dearth of sure facts: every time she thought she'd got hold of one it twisted out of her grasp. Given anything better she wouldn't have been interested in the opinion of a supposed psychic. But there was nothing else, and if it was Shad or nothing, by a short head Shad won.

Suddenly she broke eye contact, dived into her satchel. 'If I gave you something I know Philip wrote, could you say then which postcard was his?'

Shad thought, then nodded. 'Maybe.'

'Even something pretty old?'

'Probably.'

She thrust it in front of him: not a card this time but a letter, drafted in the same wild scrawl, the edges of the paper softened by the number of times it had been handled.

'Can I read it?'

'If it'll help.'

It was two years old, written from the town of Koro in the Ivory Coast. He'd been building a dam there. The letter was full of appalling puns and civil engineering jokes that Fee's pupils would have considered unsophisticated. ('Digging holes for a living is the pits.' 'The pyramids of Egypt were Africa's first major reservoir project, only the civil engineer I'm-Hopeless read the plans upside down. Pharaoh Two-Tanks-Or-None was furious.' 'When people ask what I'm here for I tell them Koronic irrigation. I don't know why they look so surprised.') There was more in the same vein: no real news, just a keeping-in-touch of two people who were plainly fond of one another.

It finished with a caricature of a thin man with a big hat and knobbly knees labouring with a shovel in the equatorial sun while a pot-bellied dog dozed in a hammock. Beneath it he'd scribbled: 'Here, even mad dogs have more sense.'

Before he got that far Shad had the answer to Fee's question. He put the letter back in its envelope and placed it in front of her. On top he laid the postcard from Edinburgh. 'Those two were written by the same man.'

*   *   *

'You want to do what?' said Dan Sale, gazing at Rosie over the top of his spectacles. They were gold wire-rimmed granny specs that didn't altogether suit his weathered face; the other thing about them was that he took them off to read. There was a general feeling at the *Chronicle* that he used them primarily to lend *gravitas* to his glares.

But Rosie was harder to intimidate than the average reporter; in fact had no idea she was meant to feel intimidated. Without waiting for an invitation she lowered herself into his visitor's chair and said it again. 'I want to take them both to Edinburgh, see what we can find out. You can do without me for a couple of days. Alex'll run the office—and you know you get fewer complaints when she answers the phone than when I do. I've got plenty of stuff set up for next week's page already, I can catch up over the weekend if I have to. It'll be quite a story if we find him. And if we don't—' She tailed off.

'If you don't?'

'I don't rightly know,' admitted Rosie. 'The

97

girl's right, something's happened to him. Even without Shad's contribution you've got a man going missing in suspicious circumstances. He had a problem, was going to visit his sister but never turned up. Now he's supposed to be bird-watching on Shetland, according to a postcard that Shad says was written by someone else. Also, the people he's working for know him under a different name, not very different, but why would he use an alias at all? And why would anybody want it to look as if he's somewhere he isn't?'

Dan wasn't glaring at her any longer but he was troubled. 'Rosie, are you telling me this man could be dead?'

Rosie rolled her eyes. 'Oh, Dan, don't even think it. There has to be another explanation. Maybe he was in trouble and he's gone into hiding. Maybe he got a friend to send the card so anyone hunting him would go to the wrong place. But Fee and her brother think the world of each other, I can't believe he'd choose to disappear without telling her first. Now somebody wants us to believe he hasn't disappeared at all. Forget Shad: *I* get bad feelings about that.'

'What do you hope to find in Edinburgh?'

She blew her cheeks out in a kind of facial shrug. 'Dan, I don't know. If I'm expecting too much of him and Shad Lucas is a good dowser and that's all, probably nothing. But if he is even marginally psychic I'd like to see what he makes of Philip Morris's lodgings.

'That's the last location we can definitely place him: we know he was there on the first of June, sitting at his desk writing to his sister. His landlady expected him to be there when she got back from a wedding, but he'd already left. He wrote to Fee that he was coming to Skipley, but something happened to change his plans. If significant events really do leave an impression on the ether, maybe Shad'll sense something.'

'And, er . . ., he's willing to do this, is he?'

Rosie gave him a puzzled frown. 'What do you mean? I haven't actually asked, but why wouldn't he?'

Dan Sale breathed heavily at her. There were times, he thought, when his newspaper's professional counsellor showed all the insight and sensitivity of a rutting hippopotamus. 'This is the same boy, is it? The one who found three dead children and put his hazel twig into cold storage for eight years? All right, maybe he feels differently now. But you're asking him to go into a room where a man may have been hurt, or worse, and it doesn't occur to you that he might refuse?'

Along with her failings, Rosie had notable strengths. One was the ability to accept fair criticism. She closed her eyes and vented a silent whistle. 'You do have a point. I'm so bloody involved in this I didn't even see it. Maybe I should forget the whole idea. Maybe I shouldn't even ask him.'

'Maybe you should ask him,' said Dan carefully, 'and shut up long enough to listen to his answer.'

It wasn't overt approval but it would do. Rosie nodded and made for the door. If she got out while she was ahead, probably he'd forget all about it until he got either her copy or her claim for expenses.

She almost made it. But as she crossed the threshold, pulling the door behind her, his voice followed her into the corridor. 'And Rosie—'

She paused. 'Dan?'

'However it works out, stay off the whisky.'

*   *   *

Everyone who knew him expected Shad Lucas to live somewhere quaint, perhaps not a painted caravan in the woods but maybe a gate lodge, a keeper's cottage, even a canal boat.

He lived in a two-room flat above a shoe-shop in Skipley High Street. He didn't even have a garden. Rosie thought Prufrock had given her the wrong address until she saw the piebald Land Rover parked outside.

But her surprise was nothing beside Shad's when he answered the insistent drilling at his bell and found Rosie on his step. 'Can I have a word?'

His living room was fourteen steep steps above the street. Rosie hauled herself up by the rail, puffing indignantly. The vicarage was full of stairs but they were wide and broken into short manageable flights. This was like climbing a ladder.

'Thing is,' she panted, dropping on to a threadbare sofa, 'Fee and I are going up to Edinburgh in the morning. We thought we'd start with the bird people, see when they last talked to Philip and where he was then, check out this story of the relief man who never turned up. And then go and see his landlady in case there's anything more she can tell us.'

Shad needed no help to know what was coming next. His voice dropped uneasily. 'Why are you telling me?'

There was no point prevaricating. He wasn't a simple rustic who could be manoeuvred into saying yes before he knew what he was agreeing to; nor did she want to do that. Dan was right: Philip Morris might have died in that room. If Shad was going to risk tuning in to that it had to be his decision.

He heard her out in absolute silence. She glanced at him from time to time but couldn't fathom what he was thinking; mostly she kept her eyes on the tweed of her skirt where it flowed over the broad Niagara of her knees. She wore tweed a lot: it was even better than washable materials because it didn't show the dirt in the first place.

When she had finished she looked at him and knew what his answer was going to be. In the split second before he could disguise it his face was appalled. 'No way. I'm sorry, but no.'

Rosie nodded. 'I understand.'

He was expecting an argument. Acceptance threw him off balance, made him try to justify himself. 'It's not that I don't want to help. But not that way. It's too much like—before. Plugging into what's left when someone's been that scared, it's—' He spent a moment searching for a way to explain.

'Finding water, that's really nice: you get this thrill of brightness and energy. You can *feel* the vitality of it. Finding lost property, a ring or a wallet, that's good, too, but not on the same scale: satisfying but pretty much the same as if it had dropped on the carpet and you'd spotted it behind a chair leg. A thing like your tyre, that's like the first twinge of toothache: not awful, just an awareness of something wrong.

'But when somebody's been hurt, or afraid, and it's been bad enough or gone on long enough to leave an impression hanging in the air afterwards, that's like—' Looking for an analogy brought a fine dew of sweat to his brow; Rosie would have stopped him if she hadn't thought he needed to tell her. 'Like drowning in electric soup.'

He blinked then, realized those were words which in the normal world had no relation to one another, that he'd have to explain the explanation. 'It's like one of those Gothick films. You're in a small room and it starts filling up with filth. You're swamped with sensations, all of them bad, and you can't stop it and you can't get out. The panic takes over. You think you're going to die in there. You think your brain's going to explode.

'It's like all the worst things you've ever heard of pumped into your head, crawling round in your synapses where you can't reach them, can't scratch them out: you've no eyes to shut and no ears to stop. The horror fills your brain. You need to get away, but by now you're too far gone even to do that. You've lost control of your limbs, of your voice; you're reduced to a trembling idiocy, a terrified child gibbering about monsters in the shadows that nobody else can see.

'Sooner or later someone takes pity on you, hauls you outside and waves his hanky in your face like you were an old lady having a fit of the vapours. Finally the flood starts to recede: the panic subsides, your wits stumble back, and he's looking at you as if you'd thrown up over his shoes. Maybe you have. This is the man you have to convince that you've something to offer. He's seen you like that, and you're asking him to spend public money digging up acres of moorland on the strength of your hunch!'

Rosie waited, but it seemed that on that unsteady note, almost like a desperate chuckle, he had finally run out of words. For a few seconds she just breathed, raggedly, trying to get a grip on herself. Oh arrogance, she thought shakily, thy name is Primrose!

She clambered out of the sofa—the springs had sagged under her weight, it was further up than it had been down—and faced him, wondering how to apologize. 'I'm sorry, I'd no business even asking. OK, so Fee's upset; but your feelings matter too.'

She saw from the flare of his eyes that he took that for blackmail, hurried to deny it. 'That sounded pretty cheap as well, didn't it? I didn't mean it like that. It's just, I hate letting people down. Oh hell, none of this is coming out the way I want, this whole bloody conversation's a minefield! Listen, I'm off now. I'm sorry if I hurt you. I'm a pushy bag when I get my teeth into something. Forget it; forget all about it. When we get back I'll let Prufrock know how we got on.'

That surprised him. 'You're still going?'

'Oh, yes. You can get more out of people face to face than over the phone. The landlady may remember something useful, and I want these bird people to commit themselves on where Philip's supposed to be. If I put the fear of God into them, maybe they'll send someone to find him. Maybe everything really is all right, he's been delayed and—' She stopped trying to convince herself. 'And if it turns out he isn't where they thought, maybe they can find out how far he got before he vanished and somebody else started writing his postcards.'

'Will Fee be angry that I'm not coming?'

'No,' said Rosie firmly. 'No, she'll understand.'

* * *

Two rings at his doorbell in one night made this a high point in Shad Lucas's social calendar. He trotted downstairs again and opened the door.

Being rather small and slightly built, Fee Morris was not physically equipped to slam the door aside, storm into the narrow hall and throw him against the wall by his shirt front. But the savage sweep of her sapphire eyes somehow created the impression that she'd done exactly that. Shad found himself stumbling back before her fury.

'Rosie says you aren't coming to Scotland tomorrow.'

'No. Yes, that's right,' he stammered, 'I'm not.'

People who didn't know her very well often likened Fee to an elf. The slight, resilient stature, the pale oval face with its acorn-cap of fair hair, the great jewel-coloured eyes, even the way she often stood half sideways as if a sudden move would startle her into flight, could create that impression. But people who knew her better thought of her as a hawk: soft downy feathers hiding talons of steel.

As if she hadn't heard him, except for that honed edge on her voice, she went on: 'I told her, No, you've got it wrong. Shad knows how important this is to me. He knows it's Philip's safety, maybe his life, we're concerned with. He wouldn't let me down. He wouldn't think digging some old biddy's rhubarb matters more than helping me find my brother. We haven't known one another long, I told her, but if he was that sort of a shit I'd have noticed!'

Shad stared at her, open mouthed, lost between anger and admiration. It was ten years since he'd spent his virginity in the shovel of a parked digger on a farmer's daughter two years older and light years more experienced than he. But somehow his sex life never lived up to this early promise. There used to be a sticker in his rent-book specifying that his flat was for single occupancy only. Somewhere along the line, though, his rent-book had been renewed and the sticker hadn't. Said it all, really, when even his landlord was aware that most of the women he knew were over sixty and too arthritic to kneel.

So he hadn't an extensive data base of girlfriends to compare her with. But instinct told him Fee Morris was special. The strength of purpose, the self-reliance, the gem-bright eyes like a fist to the solar plexus: these were not attributes commonly found in pretty young blondes. Perhaps they weren't even attributes commonly sought in pretty young blondes. But Shad Lucas felt about women much as he did about fine art: that he mightn't know anything about the subject but he knew what he liked. If he didn't know quite what he was waiting for, at least he knew what he didn't want; would rather be bullied by a girl who cared too much about something that mattered than bored by one who only cared about things that didn't.

It wasn't that he wanted to discuss politics, economics and the World Health Organisation's approach to the population crisis between the sheets; more that he wasn't interested in the news from the hairdressing salon. That actually happened to him once. He'd put his heart, body and soul into giving the girl the ride of her life; and as he came down gently from cloud nine and the noises in his ear began to make sense again, she was telling him about the difficulties of colouring your hair at home when you'd had it permed in the salon.

Shad flushed. 'This is because I won't drop everything to do what you want the minute you want it?'

'No,' she retorted fast in his face. 'It's because you won't drop everything to help a good man in trouble.'

She made it hard for him to stay angry. She was right, that was worth putting himself out for. But losing a day's work was one thing; losing his mind and his breakfast was another. 'Did Rosie say why I wouldn't come?'

She shook her head, crisply, once. 'I'm not interested in why. For reasons I don't entirely

107

understand, it seems you can help me. I'm not interested in your excuses for not doing.'

He almost hoped he would be sick. Almost, he thought it would be worth it just to see her face. His jaw came up. 'All right, I'll come to Edinburgh. I'll have a look at your brother's room, and anything I pick up I'll tell you. But I want something in return.'

She looked at him as if she'd been expecting this; down her nose, though she had to tilt her head back to do it. Her voice was icy with disdain. 'Jesus Christ, this is all I need—a psychic with the morals of an alley cat. I need something from you so I have to go in there with you first, is that it?'

Shad looked at the door she'd jerked her head at. 'That's the airing cupboard,' he lied, straight-faced. 'That's not what I'm asking. Whatever happens tomorrow, I want to see you again. That's all. Just once. After that it's up to you, but that much you owe me. I don't mind what we do—a meal, a film. There's museums and galleries in Birmingham. I'll even dance if I have to. But that's the deal. I'll come with you tomorrow, but when this is all over you'll come out with me.'

Her acorn-capped head was on one side. 'That's it? A date? Just that?'

'Just that.'

Fee thought about it, but not for long. 'All right. But I'll tell you something, Shad Lucas. Your technique's crap. If you'd asked me I'd

108

have said yes. You didn't have to make it a condition. That was cheap, and it was stupid.'

'Maybe,' he said gruffly. 'Let's see what tomorrow brings. Because if it turns out how I expect, you'd have broken a date. But I don't think you'll break a contract.'

Fee didn't understand. She shook her head abruptly, as if to dislodge something bothering her. 'We'll pick you up at eight thirty.'

'Then pick me up at Prufrock's. I can do an hour's work by eight thirty.'

CHAPTER EIGHT

Collecting Shad from Prufrock's was a mistake. When Rosie drew up outside the cottage and pipped the horn he came out with his head down, avoiding her gaze. A moment later Prufrock followed jauntily, slamming the front door behind him.

'Are we ready, then?' he asked happily. 'I'll sit in the front, shall I?—since I know Edinburgh.'

Even with motorway most of the way, three hundred miles was five hours' driving without any stops. Prufrock needed to stop several times. 'It must be the vibration,' he explained apologetically. It was after two before the crags and spires of Edinburgh appeared on the horizon.

Shad wanted to go to the house in Cowgate

109

first: he was edgy about confronting Philip Morris's disappearance in the last place he was known to have been, wouldn't relax till it was done. But Rosie had an appointment with the secretary of the British Trust for Wildlife at two thirty and didn't want to miss it. Mr Jamison had sounded reluctant to talk to her. She thought if she gave him any excuse he'd arrange a prior engagement.

Rosie never understood this effect she had on people. It had started before she was ten years old: she only had to open her mouth to turn heads. Because what came out was not childish nonsense in a piping treble but recognizably adult thought processes expressed in a clear contralto voice and punctuated with a dirty laugh.

At a time when bright girls were being guided towards teacher training or the libraries, Rosie Holland's career adviser spent an anxious weekend with a stack of leaflets and a bottle of gin before admitting that neither was a suitable profession for the woman this child was going to become and tentatively offering medicine or the army as alternatives. Rosie rather fancied herself in khaki but was sufficiently self-aware to know that army discipline would be an on-going problem. So she bought a paperback copy of *Gray's Anatomy*.

Now she was forty-seven, had succeeeded in two careers, was financially secure and had some good friends, the confidence that in a little girl had been extraordinary no longer seemed so. But still strangers reacted as if she'd just landed from Mars and she didn't know why. Rosie thought she was quite boringly normal.

Prufrock directed her through the city centre, under the shadow of the castle mount and out the other side. Then: 'Pull over, we're here.'

She did as he said, looking about her in surprise. She had expected a rural setting, a wildfowl reserve, at the very least a duck pond. But the low white building with the letters BTW and a stylized goose flying over the door was set in the sort of commercial suburb that grows up on the fringes of major cities everywhere.

The British Trust for Wildlife was a smaller operation than the name suggested. The offices made Rosie's seem spacious: if they'd trooped in together Malcolm Jamison would have had to put his filing cabinet in the back yard. They decided—or Rosie decided and no one else objected—that she and Fee would make enough of an impression on their own.

'Then can we borrow the car for half an hour?' asked Prufrock.

Rosie shrugged. 'Sure. Where are you going?'

The old man was evasive. 'Shad's never been in Edinburgh before. I thought I'd show him the sights.'

After Shad had driven away the women stood a moment on the pavement, organizing their thoughts. Now they were here, the motive for the long journey seemed less clear than it had back in Skipley. Then it had seemed the obvious next move. But what could Jamison tell them in person that he couldn't say over the phone? That Philip was living in a tent somewhere on Shetland? They'd heard that already. They'd probably have believed it but for a half-gypsy gardener who thought he could read postcards the way his mother read the tarot. Without that you just had a bird-nut who changed his mind rather a lot and found himself too long a walk from the nearest phone to keep in touch.

'Hell, Rosie,' Fee mumbled, 'I don't know about this. What am I going to say to the man? It's not his fault Philip's missing. If he is.'

'I don't suppose it is,' agreed Rosie. 'It's his fault they haven't a proper system of communications so that you can ask Philip if he's all right. It's Shetland, not Outer Mongolia! They do have telephones. They'll have a phone wherever he buys his supplies. They should have arranged regular check-in times, then if he moved on he could call in with a new number.'

Fee wrinkled her nose. 'Rosie, don't make an enemy of this man. He may not be able to help much but he's the only link I have with my brother. Maybe they could have organized things better but they're bird-watchers, not the Royal Marines. They can't have anticipated something like this.'

'They could have anticipated one of their volunteers breaking both legs falling down a cliff. Bird-watchers must do that sort of thing all the time. But if he wasn't expected to keep in contact there'd be nothing to stop him dying of exposure just because he couldn't reach the nearest phone!'

Fee paled. 'Do you think that's what's happened?'

Rosie swung between contrition and annoyance. 'Of course not: how could that explain the two cards? But it's the sort of thing BTW should have thought of. You're entitled to ask why Jamison has failed in his duty to manage his projects in a safe and efficient way. He has no right to lose touch with his watchers for weeks at a time.

'He has to understand that now the question of Philip's safety has come up it won't go away until he can show that he's on Shetland and he's OK. Insist on talking to Philip. If they really can't get a message to him, insist that somebody goes up there to find him and bring him back. It's the only way you're going to know for sure who wrote what and why—if you talk to your brother and ask him.'

Fee nodded, drew herself up to her scant full height and shouldered through the door.

Malcolm Jamison wasn't quite what they were expecting. The stereotype of a bird-watcher is so universal because it's essentially accurate. The photographs Philip sent Fee of himself and his friends about their favourite pursuit really did show windswept figures, half noticeably tall and thin and the other half noticeably short and stout, dressed in anoraks, bobble hats, beards (the men, mostly) and fell boots, with binoculars and scarves round their necks and broad adolescent grins.

By contrast, Jamison might have been a Royal Marine. He was about twenty-eight, Rosie supposed, a tall athletic man in a shirt so dazzlingly white it would have cleared the birds off ten acres of moor. There was something dazzling about him, too: the handsome clean-cut face, the blond hair, the peridot-green eyes bursting with sincerity. He met the women at his door and ushered them inside, finding them somewhere to sit. Fee got a good modern office chair upholstered in ginger tweed while Rosie got a round bentwood chair you'd think twice about putting your coat down on.

'So you're Miss Phillips,' he said affably. 'I'm sorry . . . Miss Morris. I can't get over that.' He chuckled. 'We must have entered his name wrong in the log when he first joined us and he was too polite to put us right.'

'But it is definitely my brother we're talking about?' Fee produced a photograph from her satchel.

'Oh, yes,' nodded Jamison, looking. 'That's certainly him. He's an engineer, yes?'

'That's right. And you say he's on Shetland?'

'For the Scoters,' nodded Jamison. 'Black ducks.'

'And he's been there for two months?'

'We hit a snag,' admitted the secretary. 'Someone should have relieved him three weeks ago but he let us down and Philip agreed to stay on. He's due back'—he glanced at a calendar on the wall—'in another fortnight.'

'And where, actually, is he?' asked Rosie.

Jamison did a big, handsome smile. 'Goodness, I don't know! He has a tent with him. He moves on every week or so, once he thinks he's seen everything a site has to offer. He's particularly interested in the Common Scoters this summer, but where he looks for them and how long he observes them is up to him. I wouldn't presume to advise someone with Philip's experience where he should pitch his tent and how long is long enough.'

Rosie wanted to be clear on this. 'What you're saying is, you think he's on Shetland somewhere but the last contact you had with him was three weeks ago when you asked him to stay on.'

'That's right,' Jamison agreed coolly.

'He could be anywhere!' exclaimed Rosie. 'He could have left the island. He could be sick or injured in his tent somewhere, and you don't even know where!'

Jamison frowned. 'This isn't a schoolboy we're talking about, Miss ... um ...' He'd forgotten her name, or pretended to. 'Philip Morris is an experienced observer thoroughly familiar with these conditions. Miss Morris, you know that. Half the places he works he's effectively camping out. At least there are no scorpions on Shetland.'

'Where was he when you last spoke?'

'Unst. There are Common Scoters breeding up there. Earlier he was camped near Burrafirth for a time, then at Esha Ness. He was going to try his luck on Vaila and maybe take a trip out to Foula on the ferry.' He smiled apologetically. 'So just where he is at this precise moment I really couldn't say; but in another fortnight he'll be in Lerwick for the journey home. Honestly, there's nothing to be anxious about.'

Rosie shook her head in wonder. 'How can you say that if you haven't heard from him for three weeks?'

The secretary breathed heavily at her. 'Because we hear soon enough if something goes wrong. Shetland isn't the last outpost of civilization. It's full of people—tourists, walkers, yachtsmen, other birders—quite apart from the residents. If Philip had got into trouble we'd have been contacted. Wherever he is he'll be getting supplies from a local shop, milk from a farm. If he went missing they'd raise the alarm.'

116

Turning to Fee, his green eyes warmed. 'Don't think I'm trying to put you off. I honestly think he's fine, just doing what he always does only this time he's staying a bit longer. I promise you, if I thought your brother or any of our volunteers had problems I wouldn't be sat here struggling with the accounts, I'd be on my way up there.'

Reassured somewhat, Fee nodded and tentatively smiled. Rosie said, 'When he first set off, a couple of months ago—how far in advance was that arranged?'

Jamison consulted a diary. 'A few weeks. He called to say he was going to be in The Minch for a fortnight, was there anything we wanted him to look out for? There wasn't but I said we needed someone on Shetland if he was free when he got back. He said he was and we pencilled him in.'

'Funny, that,' Rosie said mildly. 'He told Fee he was coming to visit her when he got back from The Minch.'

Jamison shrugged. 'He must have forgotten. All I know is, a fortnight later he turned up and we put him on the boat.'

'The public ferry?'

'No, in fact we took him out. We lease a boat for the season. Doing so much of our work on islands or remote strips of coast it's pretty essential.'

'It's a long haul out to the Shetlands.'

'About a hundred miles. But the boat was in

117

Scrabster and going as far as Orkney; it made more sense to send her a bit further than let Philip make his own way.'

'How's he getting back?'

Jamison smiled, not altogether nicely. 'If Interpol are waiting to interview him, perhaps he'd better fly back.'

'You think we're being neurotic, worrying about him,' stated Rosie. 'I think you're being very casual not doing.'

In the face of a direct challenge he backed down. 'Not neurotic, no. But I don't think you realize how open-ended these arrangements are, and that we work like that because it suits us. Bird-watchers like to be left alone. If we started checking up on them every week they'd tell us where to shove our binoculars. They're not interested in company. They're interested in birds.'

All of which Fee knew to be true. Last night she'd been afraid that Philip was dead, that the card hinting at trouble in Edinburgh, the other that Shad said was forged, and the uncertainty about his whereabouts bore no other interpretation. But everything Jamison said made sense, and in the cool light of day what Shad said didn't. That left only a card that was never sent, probably because it was out of date as soon as it was written. Perhaps the problem Philip hinted at had resolved itself. Or perhaps he'd gone to Shetland to leave it behind.

Either way she'd over-reacted. She'd

dragged herself and three other people three hundred miles only to hear a perfectly lucid account of where Philip was and why he couldn't be contacted at short notice. She started to rise. 'I think we've put you to quite enough trouble, Mr Jamison.'

Behind his desk Jamison rose, too. 'Think nothing of it. I understand why you were alarmed: I'm glad I've been able to set your mind at rest. As soon as we hear from him I'll have him call you. You'll be going home soon?'

'Tonight,' she said. 'I'll leave you my number.' She scribbled it on the pad he offered; as an afterthought she added her address.

'Fine,' said the secretary. 'If you can be patient for another fortnight I'm confident he'll have called by then.'

Rosie was less satisfied than Fee by the answers they'd been given, and wasn't at all embarrassed about putting people to trouble. 'Will there be someone to take over from him?'

Jamison seemed to resent Rosie's part in this. His brows lowered in a shadow of a frown. 'In fact, no. With one of the volunteers dropping out we haven't been able to maintain a full programme this summer. We're not a big set-up, as you may have noticed.'

Rosie nodded. 'Running a boat big enough to hop out to the Shetlands must be quite a drain on your resources, then.'

He shrugged. 'Buying a new pair of

binoculars is quite a drain on our resources, but without them we might as well shut up shop.'

Fee already had the door open. 'Thanks for your time, Mr Jamison. I'd appreciate hearing as soon as Philip checks in.'

'Of course, Miss Morris. The moment I hear from him.'

'And if we get any news first,' Rosie said cheerfully, 'we'll call you.'

Jamison's expression froze. 'News?'

'Yes. Most of Philip's friends watch birds, too. A few people offered to go to Shetland if he didn't turn up soon.'

'Ah,' said Malcolm Jamison. 'Yes? Fine. There'll be no need, of course. I'm sure Miss Morris will hear from her brother before long.'

'I do hope so,' said Rosie, holding his eye.

CHAPTER NINE

There was no sign of the car so they stood on the pavement arguing. Rosie thought Fee had allowed herself to be sweet-talked. Fee thought Rosie wanted an exposé to justify her time and petrol.

'Jesus Christ!' yelled Rosie in exasperation. 'Yesterday—only yesterday—you were ready to do whatever it took to find Philip and bring him home. You came to me, remember? You were scared, you didn't know where to turn, the police couldn't help you, and you came to me because I was prepared to try. How dare you accuse me of bylining? We'd none of us be here if it wasn't for you. You practically abducted Shad. But one flash of starry-eyed sincerity from the golden boy in there and that's fine, Mr Jamison; I'm sure everything's all right, Mr Jamison; if you say so Mr Jamison; turn round, Mr Jamison, and I'll kiss—'

'Rosie!' The car cruised to a halt beside them, with Prufrock hanging out of the nearside window. 'Have we kept you waiting?'

'No,' said Fee, tight-lipped, 'you came at just the right time.' She climbed into the back seat.

Actually, Rosie rather thought so, too. She changed the subject. 'Where've you been—the castle?'

'Arthur's idea of the sights of Edinburgh differs from most people's,' murmured Shad. He went to give up the wheel but Rosie waved him back: she'd been driving all morning, was glad of a break. With a little encouragement Prufrock vacated the front passenger seat. 'We've been touring vendors of outdoor clothing.'

Prufrock chuckled in his moustache. 'My young friend is being deliberately obtuse. We have indeed visited two such emporia, and a gun shop, but only because that's where the people I wanted to talk to work.'

Straight-faced, Rosie said, 'Bird-watchers?'

Prufrock nodded, unaware that she was mocking him. 'Some of the people I called

121

when I was first looking for Philip. I thought it would be nice to introduce myself and say thanks.'

'And . . .' prompted Shad.

The old man was sanguine. 'And to see what else they could tell me. About Philip; about how these surveys are organised; about the British Trust for Wildlife and your Mr Jamison.'

'He's not my Mr Jamison,' growled Rosie. She stopped short of adding, 'He's Fee's,' but only just. 'Anything useful?'

Prufrock wasn't sure. He'd enjoyed himself, meeting people of similar interests and wheedling information out of them, but it was hard to know how much of what he'd learned would be of any help. Mr Polly who sold climbing equipment, Miss Threadgoode who specialized in wax waterproofs and Mr Monk who sold and serviced guns all knew and liked Philip Morris, found him easy to get on with but serious enough about the job to do it properly. The suggestion that he was travelling from rock to blighted rock counting birds raised no eyebrows. They thought he was the perfect choice.

'As Miss Threadgoode said, the last thing you need on a serious survey is some twitcher who's only interested in rarities. Scientific observation requires you to watch whatever's there, LBJs as well as the weird and wonderful,' said Prufrock.

'LBJs?'

'Little Brown Jobs.'

'So there was nothing odd about BTW sending him to Shetland?'

Prufrock frowned. 'Nothing odd about them sending Philip, no. They were a little surprised that he'd been sent to Shetland. There are two nature reserves on the islands—summer visitors squatting in a tent aren't likely to add much to the information they can gather. Since BTW has a boat in Oban, mostly they concentrate on the west coast.'

'The boat was in Scrabster, apparently, going out to the Orkneys. They just sent it a bit further.'

'On the north coast?' Prufrock didn't understand. 'That's a long way from Oban. It must have taken them a couple of days to get there. And why? Public ferries serve Orkney and Shetland, they wouldn't need their own boat up there. You could buy a season ticket on the ferry for the cost of the diesel you'd burn getting it there.'

Rosie's interest quickened. 'What about BTW? What's their reputation like?'

'A bit mixed. There may be a degree of chauvinism there, even a sprinkling of jealousy. Jamison's not short of money. There are long-standing, well respected ornithology groups round here that have trouble keeping their hides weather-proof, and in comes this Englishman with his big ideas and his big chequebook, and before they know it he's got his own boat. So we might take their criticisms with a pinch of salt.'

'What criticisms?'

Geoffrey Monk in the gun shop had said the least and conveyed the most. Since he was a mild, rather colourless man with polite manners and a mission to please it was all the more noticeable that he hadn't a good word for the British Trust for Wildlife. He even seemed to find them a little dubious.

'Came from nowhere, Mr Prufrock,' he said. 'I'd never heard of them, neither had any of the birders I've talked to. They don't use local volunteers, unless you count Philip and even he's English—though mostly we've forgiven him for that by now. And they don't show any interest in anyone else's activities. Any time there's a joint venture BTW is conspicuous by its absence. It raises hackles, Mr Prufrock. It's not how bird-people behave, you know that. We muck in, we don't keep to ourselves.'

Rosie indicated the building behind them. 'Did you ask him about Jamison personally?'

'I did,' said Prufrock. 'Mr Monk clammed up. He said he knew nothing to his detriment, but in such a way as to raise whole clouds of suspicion.'

That might have had more to do with Monk himself than Jamison. He was a younger man than Prufrock; they'd never met or even spoken over the phone until this business began, but

124

Prufrock had a clear picture of the sort of man he was—a natural conservative, a man who'd lived and worked all his life in one place, a man whose twin ambitions were paying off his mortgage and seeing an Alpine Accentor. He was the sort of man who would quite naturally take against the sort of man Malcolm Jamison seemed to be.

'He wouldn't even say he didn't like him; but then again, he didn't have to. What did you make of Jamison? Was he able to explain at all? Does he know where Philip is?'

Fee nodded. 'He says so. I'm inclined to believe him, Rosie isn't.'

Rosie scowled. 'Who am I to say—I'm only here for the headlines. If you're satisfied we can go home right now.'

An argument between women was like a squabble between small boys: easier to make worse than better. Prufrock debated a moment. 'We've come a fair way, maybe we should at least visit Mrs Mackey before we leave. She is expecting us.'

Mrs Mackey didn't know what to make of them. She'd always thought Philip a bit odd, but compared with his friends and relations he seemed the model of convention.

There was the sister. Sweet little thing, you thought, until she caught your eye and you found yourself backing into the furniture. The face of a child, the body of an adolescent, the eyes of a panther and a handshake like a

125

Glasgow trucker.

There was the sister's friend. Mrs Mackey had no time for this cult of thinness, she fed her son and lodgers as if fattening them for slaughter, so she appreciated a woman of substance with apple cheeks, an ample bosom and a lap sufficient to accommodate three under-fives at a time. But though all the equipment was in place, in Primrose Holland the effect was anything but maternal. It wasn't even the casual saltiness of her language—Mrs Mackey had heard worse from women with children like storage jars, one in each size—so much as the authoritative way she spoke, as if she were used to being heeded. Mothers don't sound like that.

There was the old man. He knew the city, which counted for something, but he wasn't a Scot and when he said he'd taught in a private school in Argyll she found herself nodding as if she should have guessed. There was a tidiness about him, almost a prissiness, that set Mrs Mackey's teeth on edge. The late Mr Mackey was a welder; Mrs Mackey's father was a miner. She couldn't help it, she found gratuitous cleanliness in a man sinister.

Finally, there was the young man. Miss Morris introduced him as Ms Holland's friend but Mrs Mackey had her doubts. There was something too deliberate about the way the young people didn't look at one another. That wasn't genuine lack of interest—they were

126

putting it on, each unaware that the other was doing the same. Mrs Mackey reckoned to know a bit about matters of the heart, thought they looked a promising couple, couldn't think why they were being so coy. Neither had a ring on. The girl was pretty (if you didn't mind thin) and the boy, despite some rough edges, seemed decent enough. So far as Mrs Mackey could see they were a good match.

And then Shad Lucas said through his teeth, 'If I start foaming at the mouth, get me outside. That's all. Don't panic, don't call an ambulance, just get me outside. I'll be all right. Just don't for Christ's sake leave me in there.'

At which point Mrs Mackey regretted her promise to show them Philip's room. It had been empty for ten weeks now, give or take a day, and this morning the landlady spent an hour cleaning it. Now it seemed she was giving a conducted tour to a party of mad people.

But it was too late to change her mind so she showed them in. 'It's lovely this time of year,' she said, as if they were prospective tenants. 'I just wish I'd time to do up the garden. This used to be the drawing-room—lovely big room . . .' She ran out of things to say and fell silent.

Rosie said, 'Is this how Philip left it? You haven't taken advantage of his absence to make some changes?'

She meant no criticism but Mrs Mackey bristled at the suggestion that she might take advantage of anyone. 'This is Mr Morris's room, it's how he likes it, it'll stay this way until I hear from him that he wants it different.'

Rosie realized she'd given offence, unintentionally for once, but it would take too long to explain. 'OK, fine. Shad?'

'Yeah.' For a couple of heartbeats he hesitated, then he stepped over the threshold into the room.

There was nothing extravagant about the house but Mrs Mackey had long ago discovered that buying good furniture secondhand was better, both financially and aesthetically, than buying cheap furniture new. The resultant aura of slightly worn gentility was both comfortable and pleasing.

Beside the tall window was the desk, a row of books along the back. Rosie looked at the spines. Ornithology, engineering and rather juvenile humour. 'The book the postcard was in—was it one of these?'

Mrs Mackey nodded stiffly. 'It was lying on the desk. He must have been reading it and never put it away.' She passed her eye along the row, selected a well-used tome on birds. It opened automatically in her hand. 'That's right, the Little Owl. I remember he was reading about the little owl.'

'What?' Prufrock's pink face creased in puzzlement and he put the emphasis on the diminutive as if it made no sense. 'The *Little* Owl?'

Rosie took the book from Mrs Mackey,

128

noting where the page had been bruised by the thickness of the card folded into it. 'That's what it says. Why?'

'Because if he was on his way to the Shetlands it's the last thing he'd have been reading up. The Little Owl, *Athene noctua*, is essentially a bird of middle England. It was introduced to the Midlands from the continent a hundred-odd years ago, since when it's spread across England into Wales and as far as the Scottish borders. But not as far north as the Shetlands.'

'So the night before he left for Shetland, according to Jamison, Philip sat here reading about birds of the Midlands for all the world as if he was going to Skipley instead.' There was a definite edge on Rosie's voice.

Fee shrugged. 'Maybe he got diverted—started reading up the Scoters, skimmed on to other things.'

Prufrock ducked his head to look at the title. 'This is a damn good book. He should have had it with him.'

Rosie had been holding it for a minute now and it was beginning to tell. 'Too heavy to lug around?'

'He wasn't walking to Shetland! And he was going to be weeks on his own—he'd need something substantial to read.' Prufrock took it from her, leafed through it, peered closely at the pages and then up-ended and shook it. Fine sand dusted the desk. Mrs Mackey bit her tongue. 'Look at that. He took it to the Hebrides. Why leave it at home this time?'

Home? That stabbed Fee like a tiny knife. This was her brother's home, the only one he'd had for four years. As a rented room there was nothing wrong with it. For a student, going back to the family every few weeks and with the promise of something better once he was working, it would be a perfectly satisfactory base of operations for months at a time.

But Philip wasn't a student and he hadn't been here for months. Excepting his time abroad he'd been here for four years. Had he been too comfortable to move, too lazy—too poor? Fee really didn't know. When he told her he lived in the shadow of Edinburgh Castle she hadn't imagined this.

'Well,' said Rosie, 'if the postcard was in the book and the book was on the desk, this is probably where Philip wrote it. Would that be a good place to start, Shad?'

Mrs Mackey watched in trepidation, wondering what it was that Shad was going to start at the desk of her best room. But all he did was pull out the chair and sit down. He put something down on the blotter—the postcard?—and after a moment reached into the neck of his shirt for something else. Mrs Mackey thought it was a medallion, but it was a piece of silver pecked into a leaf shape and threaded on a thong.

Rosie leaned closer, peering. 'What *is* that?'

Absently, his mind already elsewhere, Shad explained. 'It's cast from a Neolithic flint arrowhead. My uncle gave it me when he taught me how to do this. I tried different things—twigs, rods, a crystal on a chain—but this worked best so I've stuck with it.'

'How does it work?'

Shad spared her a brief, harried look. 'Beats me.'

Though she had insisted he come, Fee didn't know what to expect either. Would he dance, chant or prostrate himself on the rug? Would he moan and swing the silver charm in hypnotic circles until his eyes turned over in his head and he fell off the chair, twitching? Would he in fact foam at the mouth? 'Should we leave? While you . . . I don't know . . . make contact?'

He threw her a worried scowl. 'You got me into this, you can damn well see it through.'

Seated at Philip Morris's desk, with the postcard in front of him, Shad opened his hand and let the arrowhead drop the length of its thong to swing gently above the scrawl of words. His eyes softened and slid out of focus, his breathing steadied and slowed. The silver leaf did not begin to pendulum wildly, nor did it fall entirely still: it continued to describe a small, unhurried circle above the skew-whiff portrait of Her Majesty.

And that was all. No drama; no sudden revelations; no foaming; no fits. They waited— Fee who was desperate for news of her brother,

131

Prufrock who was anxious for Shad, Rosie who wanted almost any answers to any of several questions, and Mrs Mackey who was worried about her furniture—for minutes while nothing happened. Behind Shad's back Fee cast Rosie a puzzled look and Rosie replied with a shrug.

Mrs Mackey mouthed, 'I'll get on with my dusting.'

When Shad finally gathered the arrowhead into his hand and stood up the movement was so unexpected that Fee started and Rosie gasped 'What? What?' as if she'd nodded off. Prufrock let out a ragged breath as if he'd been holding it all that time.

'OK,' said Shad with a faint smile. He looked pale but calm; searching his face Rosie found no signs of distress. 'Do you want the good news or the bad news?'

Fee's eyes roasted him. 'If you've something to tell me, tell me.'

Only mildly chastened, Shad nodded. 'The good news is, nobody's died in this room—not ever so far as I can make out. Whatever happened, it wasn't that. But he was worried when he was writing that card: there's a real anxiety that I'm picking up. And something else, I'm not sure what—another person?'

'Not Mrs Mackey?'

'No. I can feel her but she's different. I think this was another man. There was—an argument? I'm not sure.'

'A fight?' prompted Rosie.

Shad shook his head. 'I don't think so. There isn't—enough. There isn't enough of anything.' With a little shrug he gave up. 'This isn't being much help, is it?'

'It's helping me,' Fee said, looking straight at him. 'Look, I think I've brought you all on a wild-goose chase. I'm sorry about that. All I can say is, I genuinely believed Philip was in trouble. I was afraid he'd come to some harm, that he was dead, even. That card you said he didn't write: I couldn't think of any other explanation.

'But you also said you could be wrong about that, and now I really think you were. I think Jamison was right. These places he goes, nobody could keep in regular touch. Something was worrying him, he wasn't going to go, then he got it sorted and he went; and he wrote from Shetland to say he was OK. Maybe he wrote twice and the first card went astray. That's all there is to it. No mystery, no drama. You're not picking up anything sinister because there's nothing to pick up.'

Shad said softly, 'If you believe I can tell that your brother didn't die here, why don't you believe I can tell that he didn't write that postcard?'

Fee had no answer to that. She just said in a low voice, 'I'm sorry I've wasted your time. We had a deal: I'll stick by it if you want me to. I can do that, and I can pay for Rosie's petrol, and I can apologize, and that's all I can do. Now can we please go home?'

Through her teeth Rosie said, 'That's it? We're finished? We haven't found Philip, we haven't found anyone who's seen him in more than two months, but Malcolm Jamison says everything's all right so we pack up and go home. Jesus, he could have said that over the phone!'

'All right,' snapped Fee, rounding on her, 'why are you so determined *not* to believe him? Just because we've come so far? That's my fault, not his. Dear God, I think you *want* Philip to be dead, if only to prove you right!'

Rosie levelled a finger under her nose. 'Say that to me once more, Fiona Morris, and you're going to wake up with a crowd round you.'

Prufrock intervened with a shocked expression, pink hands flapping. 'Ladies, ladies! Please! I'm sure we're all doing our best, let's not fall out about it. At least, not in this good lady's house. Are we finished here? Can we go back to the car to discuss our next move?'

Shad shrugged. 'I'm finished.' Fee nodded. After a moment Rosie did, too.

Fee called Mrs Mackey in from the hall. 'Philip should be back in a couple of weeks. If he'll owe you rent before that I can leave you a cheque.'

Once again Mrs Mackey bridled. 'Your brother has been my good tenant, indeed my friend, for four years. It'll be a sad day that I can't trust him for a month's rent.' She glared round them, daring them to contradict. No one did.

But when her eye lit on Shad and took in the hard muscles under his shirt an idea occurred to her and her tone altered. 'You wouldn't do something for me before you go? This window's been sticking ever since the man came to fix the glass. My son tried to free it but he's only twelve, he could only shift it a couple of inches. You wouldn't give it a good heave for me?'

'Sure.' That was the sort of request Shad preferred—taxing his body was easier than taxing his mind. He went to the window, inserted strong fingers into the gap underneath and straightened his back.

For a second it resisted; then suddenly it broke free and shot above his head, admitting a summer breeze ripe with the smell of the overgrown garden.

But that gentle zephyr hit Shad with the force of a hurricane. He gave a startled squawk and stumbled back three or four paces, then tripped and sat down on the rug. His eyes saucered.

'There,' he exclaimed, nodding energetically at the window. 'Outside. That's why I could hardly feel the other man. He was never in the room, he was outside the window. He broke the glass. With . . . with . . .' Still sitting on the rug, trying to make sense of the half-coded snatch of information he'd received, like a fragment torn from a snapshot, he was echoing the

135

movement unconsciously with his hand. 'A rock
. . . a hammer?'

But any child big enough to reach the
buttons on a TV would have recognized the
distinctive shape formed by his fingers. If it had
been a rock he'd have broken the glass with his
knuckles; if it had been a hammer his thumb
would have been wrapped round it, not stuck
up in the air like that.

Rosie wasn't a TV addict but when she did
watch she liked something fast moving and
rather trashy, with a good measure of
gratuitous violence—the sort of thing people
write to the Broadcasting Complaints
Commission about. One of the earliest letters
to *The Primrose Path* came from a woman
concerned that her nine-year-old's exposure to
shootings, stabbings and explosions would turn
him into a psychopath. 'I shouldn't think so,'
Rosie had replied, 'it hasn't me.'

Shad didn't watch a lot of television, apart
from the gardening programmes, so he missed
the significance of that up-raised thumb. But
the nine-year-old wouldn't have done and
neither did Rosie. She said softly, 'What about
a gun?'

CHAPTER TEN

'Tell us about the window,' Rosie said quietly.

If Mrs Mackey hadn't seen it happen she
wouldn't have believed it. But she had seen it:

136

had seen a sturdy young man flung halfway across the room by—well, so far as she could see, by nothing. It might have been a pretence but it didn't look like it. She was beside him when it happened, and his look of wide-eyed astonishment was exactly the same as if a passing bishop had knocked him down with his crook. If he could act like that he was wasted doing anything else.

'It was the day Philip was here.' Her voice was reedy with shock; Prufrock steered her to a chair and sat her down solicitously. 'Ian and I were at my niece's wedding in Perth. We left mid-morning and weren't back till late. I knew Philip was due back from The Minch but he could never say exactly when.

'When we got back about eleven there was a light on in here. I thought he was home so put my head in to say hello. But he wasn't here. He'd *been* here—he'd left his laundry, and a note for me about the broken window with some money pinned under the lamp. I tacked a bit of cardboard over the hole and the next day I got the man out from the glaziers. He must have left a bit of putty in the sash, though, because the window hasn't opened properly since. Until—' Lacking words to describe it she nodded in Shad's direction.

Shad had recovered quickly. Rosie helped him to his feet and sat him on the edge of Philip's bed; but he wasn't faint, wouldn't put his head between his knees, and within a

137

minute he was on his feet and prowling the room.

Fee stood open-mouthed, with shock or disbelief, and when Shad could sit still no longer she took his place on the bed. 'What do we do?' she whispered.

Rosie took a deep breath. 'I think, and I don't offer the suggestion with any enthusiasm, we tell the police.'

Mrs Mackey directed them to the police station in St Leonards Street where they were seen by a detective sergeant. They all went. Fee was the missing man's brother, Shad the witness—if that was the right word—to what was apparently an attack on him, and Prufrock might be needed as an interpreter. Rosie never even wondered if her own presence was called for.

Detective Sergeant Rush took them to an interview room, an amiable man of middle-age trying to hide what was passing through his mind. He listened without interruption, made a few notes, asked why they thought a gun was involved and didn't laugh when Shad said that was it: he thought it, there was no why or wherefore. Prufrock explained about the Clee Hills and Rush jotted down the name of the senior officer concerned. After that they all sat in silence for a minute.

'You'll appreciate,' Rush said then, 'I can't set up an Incident Room on the strength of a psychic experience, however impressive Mr

Lucas's track record. What I will do is open a file on Mr Morris so that any information that could be relevant will reach me. And I'll contact the police in Lerwick, ask them to look for him. I gather you'd be happier, Miss Morris, if you knew your brother had definitely reached Shetland?'

Fee nodded.

'Right, I'll see what I can do. Where will you be in the next day or two, if I've any news?'

'I'll be at home,' said Fee.

'And I'll be staying with Mrs Mackey in Cowgate,' said Rosie briskly, taking them all by surprise.

Mrs Mackey was pretty surprised, too, but supposed she could find a room in the circumstances.

'Er ... could you find two?' ventured Prufrock.

He got a bed-settee in the little guest room in the attic; Rosie moved into Philip's room. She wanted Fee to stay, too, but Fee was afraid she'd miss a vital call from her brother or someone who knew something about him if she wasn't at home to take it.

'Besides, what more can I do here? I'd have gone to Shetland if there was any point, but if he got there he's probably all right. If he didn't get there, maybe he never got much further than this room. I can't stay here. I'll call the station, find out when there's a train.'

'Shad?'

Shad was watching Fee, unaware that everyone in the room knew it. He hunched his shoulders in an unhappy shrug. 'She can't go alone. I'll go, too. I don't know how much more I can do here either.'

Perhaps nothing, but Rosie would have liked him to stay just in case. But he was right, Fee was too upset to make the five-hour journey alone; and maybe he needed to get away as much as she did. Rosie nodded. 'All right, you two get yourselves back home. Arthur and I'll stay for a day or two, see if anything more turns up. If not we'll come back at the weekend.'

There was a train out of Waverley Station just after five; they made it by the skin of their teeth. Rosie and Prufrock waved them out of sight, mainly because that's what you do on station platforms. When the train was only a rattle in the distance Prufrock said, 'Turn up? Such as what?'

Rosie shrugged. 'I dunno. I'd like another crack at Jamison; and to talk to the crew of his boat. If Philip got as far as Shetland they're the last people we know of who saw him. But if Shad's right and something happened to him here then Jamison's lying, he never reached Scrabster. I wonder how helpful Jamison will be when I ask to talk to the crew?'

Prufrock frowned. 'You don't trust him, do you? Why not?'

Rosie wriggled her shoulders. 'I don't know. He's a smug bastard but that doesn't mean he's
140

lying. It would only take Shad to be mistaken, and he never claimed to be foolproof. Maybe something did happen but it wasn't that: some kids kicked a ball over the wall, say, and broke the window that way. That might have startled Philip enough to leave an impression in the room without it meaning anything sinister. Do you think that's possible? That because we were anxious Shad sensed a conspiracy where none existed?'

Prufrock nodded. 'Certainly. When I was first aware of this talent of his I did some reading. What dowsers seem to do is put a fine edge on guesswork. A Welsh expert experimenting with map-dowsing for the Society of Psychical Research got a result four times out of ten. That's a lot better than random chance—it was no easy task, he was in London dowsing for megaliths in America—but he was still wrong more often than he was right. So yes, Shad could certainly be wrong, in substance or in detail.

'It's important, Rosie, that we keep this in perspective. It's an extraordinary gift, but it isn't something to stake your reputation on. I saw what happened, too, and I'm sure he wasn't making that up. But what was it he sensed? We know what it looked like, we drew a certain conclusion, but we don't know and he doesn't know what it *was*.

'It's not like being an eye-witness. At best it's a hint of what may have happened. Knowing

141

his history we can't ignore it, but we should treat it with caution. If we don't and we're wrong, we're going to make fools of ourselves. That doesn't matter too much, we've probably both done it before. But making a fool of Shad does matter. This thing has had him close to the edge in the past. I don't want that happening again.'

He was right, of course. What a psychic was good for, in a forensic sense, was leaping gaps in the evidence to find a trail after it seemed broken and lost; as a tool of investigation, not a substitute for it. Like a sniffer dog, which within its limitations was an indispensable member of a police team. But if a search of the person or property it indicated yielded no drugs you couldn't ask the dog to testify to what it had detected. The sniffer dog, and the psychic, could give investigators information they could obtain no other way, but the case had to be made by conventional means.

If there really was a man with a gun perhaps Philip Morris was dead; but his remains would eventually be discovered. As a pathologist Rosie knew how hard the human body resists dissolution. Sometime, somewhere, he would be found and would speak out against his murderer. Or if he were not dead, perhaps he was indeed on Shetland and the Lerwick police would soon set everyone's mind at rest.

But the boatmen knew now, if they would tell her. If Jamison would contact them for her.

They caught him leaving the office. He locked the door behind him and strolled over to his car: a white Range Rover, Rosie noticed without surprise. Highly suitable for the places an ornithologist would go; as Shad's Land Rover would have been. Prufrock's friends might be jealous but they were also right: this tiny operation had an inordinate amount of money to spend.

As Jamison settled himself in the big car Rosie leaned an elbow on his windowsill. 'Hello again.'

A range of emotions flitted across his face, chief among them a wholly gratifying dismay. 'It's Miss . . . um . . .'

'Holland,' she supplied, a little like a tiger introducing itself to a tethered goat. 'Ms. And this is my friend Mr Prufrock. My other friend Miss Morris is on her way home to wait for her brother's call. But do you know, I think she could wait a long time? I thought I'd stay here and see what else I could find out. From you, for instance.'

Jamison gave her a hunted look. 'What makes you think there's something I'd tell you that I wouldn't tell her?'

'Ah,' said Rosie. 'Well, because she thinks it would be impolite to suggest you might have been fibbing. So do I, actually: the difference is, I don't care.'

Jamison grinned at that: a handsome grin that only irritated Rosie more. 'You could be

143

right; but in fact you're not. There's nothing more I can tell either of you.'

Rosie didn't waste time arguing. 'Where's the boat?'

That hit him hard. He actually stammered. 'B-boat?'

'Your boat. The British Trust for Wildlife boat. The boat that ferries your volunteers out to obscure off-shore islets inaccessible by any other means. Like Orkney and Shetland,' she said, heavily ironic. 'That's usually based in Oban but happened to be two days away in Scrabster when Philip Morris was there. That boat. Where is it now?'

'Why?'

She chuckled vindictively. 'Oh, wrong answer, Mr Jamison! Someone with nothing to hide would have said, "Oban. Why?"'

'I don't know where it is.'

At that she laughed out loud. 'You really aren't very good at this at all, are you? You're leasing it, Mr Jamison, BTW is paying for every litre of diesel it burns. And you don't know where it is? Pull the other one: it not only has bells attached, it plays "White Christmas"!'

'Boats don't run on rails,' he explained, as if to a child. 'Once at sea it's hard to say exactly where they are. Now *why*?'

'Because I want to talk to the skipper. He does have a radio, I presume? Every piddling little yacht in the country has a radio these days. What's the boat's name, how do I raise

144

her?'

But Jamison had had time to recover his composure, to realize he didn't actually have to answer her questions. He might have an obligation to Fee but to Rosie he had none. 'Ms Holland, I don't know what it is you suspect me of. You've no reason to suspect me of anything. In any event I'm not sitting here being brow-beaten any longer.

'If you think I've abducted Philip Morris and sold him to white slavers from one of the less discriminating South American republics, and you have some evidence to support the theory, you should tell the police. If they want to talk to me I'll be happy to co-operate; if they want our skipper to check his bilges for incriminating material—Philip's binoculars, perhaps, smelling of chloroform and with a book of matches from a Buenos Aires nightclub tucked inside—they'll know how to go about it.

'But if you want my help, Ms Holland, you can come back here tomorrow morning in a pleasanter frame of mind and ask for it.' He put the car into gear and left Rosie fuming in the middle of the road.

Prufrock waited a diplomatic moment before observing, apparently to the sky, 'There's more than one way to skin a cat.'

'And you, of course—' Realizing she had no cause to be angry with him she took a deep breath and smiled. 'And you, I suppose, wrote

145

the *Alternative Cat-skinner's Handbook.*'

He had no difficulty taking that as a compliment. People always thought of schools as places where children learned from adults; but there was a lot a grown man with an open mind could learn from forty years' worth of boys. When it came to deviousness, Machiavelli could take lessons from an elderly schoolmaster.

'If a six-inch rock bunting lands on a stone wall in Dorset, every birder in the country knows about it instantly. You think we can't find a seagoing boat?'

By then the gun shop was closed. Prufrock headed for the nearest phone-box, emerging after some minutes with a smug expression. 'He lives in Cramond. He says to go round.'

Rosie frowned. 'Who does?'

'Mr Monk who owns the gun shop. I knew he couldn't live too far away and there aren't that many Monks in Edinburgh.'

Supplying guns to decimate one class of birdlife struck Rosie as an odd occupation for someone whose hobby was observing another, but it was clearly profitable. Geoffrey Monk's house in the quiet, prosperous village of Cramond attested to the fact. It was seven o'clock when they arrived but the summer sun was still high and Monk was mowing the grass with a lawn tractor.

He drove to meet them, asked them up to the house for a drink, but Prufrock was

146

reluctant to impose on him any more and got down to business. 'That boat of BTW's. It's based in Oban?'

Monk looked momentarily taken aback; then he thought and nodded. He was a man of about forty, a bird-watcher of the tallish thinnish variety with light brown hair growing a little sparse on top. A sandpit and paddling-pool at the top of the garden identified him as a family man. 'So I believe. They seem to operate mostly around The Minch, between the Hebrides and the mainland.'

'What size of a thing is it?'

Monk shook his head. 'I've never seen it. I'm not a great connoisseur of boats.'

Prufrock pursed his lips. 'Can you think of anyone who would know it, at least by name? We're trying to contact the crew, and Mr Jamison is being less than helpful.'

The seller of guns combed his memory. 'I have heard the name somewhere. Keep talking, it'll come back. Why do you want to talk to the crew?'

'We're still looking for Philip Morris,' said Prufrock. 'Jamison says the BTW boat took him to Shetland. We're not convinced that's the truth, wondered if the crew could help.'

'They're not likely to call their employer a liar!'

'No,' agreed Rosie. 'Unless Jamison's playing his own game in some way and they don't know they're meant to back him.'

147

'What sort of game?'

'Hell, *I* don't know,' exclaimed Rosie. 'Let's see—boats, remote rocky islets miles from civilization—could they be smuggling something?'

'Without the crew's knowledge?'

'Ah,' said Rosie, acknowledging the flaw. 'No. OK, if they're up to something they're probably in it together. That doesn't mean they've got their story straight. If the crew come up with a different version from Jamison's, maybe Detective Sergeant Rush will stop looking at us as if we've given our care attendant the slip, and investigate.'

Monk looked alarmed. 'The police are involved?'

'Not that you'd notice,' sighed Rosie. 'Look, you know most of it. Philip's missing, his sister's worried sick, to be honest I am too, and Prufrock's gardener—don't even ask where he fits in!—found evidence in Philip's lodgings that he was abducted. So we told the police, who listened politely, and that was about it. But if I can get the people at BTW to contradict one another, maybe Rush'll want to know why they're lying.'

'And'—Monk looked around nervously, as if they might spring out of the rhododendrons—'where are Philip's sister and this gardener now?'

'They've gone back home to wait for news. The girl couldn't take much more and we didn't

148

want to put her on the train alone. Arthur and I thought we'd stay and see what we could find out. Finding that boat and talking to the crew seemed a good start but we'll need to do it quickly, before Jamison can cover himself. He's nobody's fool. If we give him half an inch he'll crawl through it.'

'*White Heather!*' Monk said suddenly. 'The boat's called *White Heather*. I knew I'd remember if I thought long enough. There'll be a harbour office or something in Oban. Come inside while we check the phone-book.'

Mrs Monk made them some coffee while her husband was on the phone. He came back beaming. 'Well, the piermaster came up trumps. *White Heather*'s in Oban now and she'll be there overnight. The skipper's called Haldane. The piermaster offered to have him ring but I thought perhaps you wouldn't want that, that you might prefer to go and see him. In which case it'd be better if he didn't know you were coming.'

Rosie kept a straight face. Monk clearly thought he'd walked on to the set of a spy film, was having a wonderful time. He must have forgotten that the helpful informant was always the first to get pulped.

Prufrock saw her thinking something she'd be better not saying and moved smoothly into the gap. 'Excellent. How far is Oban—three hours' drive? We could get there tonight but we'd have to stay over.'

Rosie gave a decisive nod. 'If we get there after ten we'll probably catch them with a couple of drinks inside them. So much the better. The skipper's called Haldane, you say? Did you ask what *White Heather* looks like?'

'She's a fishing boat, fifty feet long and painted white. If you go to the Railway Quay they'll point her out.'

Rosie nodded her approval. 'You're very good at this, Mr Monk. If you ever want a change from the gun shop you could be a private detective.'

Pleased, Monk blushed.

They picked up the motorway near Linlithgow and followed it west until it gave way to a slower road edging northwards. Rosie drove in near silence. Prufrock had known her just long enough to know this wasn't her natural state. 'What's on your mind?'

'I'm just wondering how long it'll take Jamison to realize we don't have to go back to him cap in hand in the morning—that we can get the information other ways. That we could, in fact, be doing what we're doing now.'

'You think we could reach Oban only to see the stern of the *White Heather* disappearing down the Firth of Lorn?'

'Yes. Or find a reception committee.' She scowled. 'I wish Shad was with us.'

Prufrock raised his eyebrows. 'You're expecting trouble? Oban's still part of the United Kingdom, Rosie, it isn't a one-cow town

150

in the Wild West! If there are problems we'll call the local constabulary. Anyway, who do you think Shad is, Arnold Swarzer . . . Swarzer . . . Errol Flynn?'

'I think he's a fit young man who probably knows how to use himself. In marked contrast, I feel obliged to point out, to us. I'm middle-aged and fat, and you're old and little. Our only chance in a showdown is if the other side die laughing.'

Prufrock didn't know whether to be amused or offended. In the end he just said, 'Nothing will happen to us in Oban, Rosie, I give you my word.' And he was absolutely right.

Where the ribbon of road threaded the dim tunnel of the Strathyre Forest, with the river glinting on the left and the trees thickening to blackness on the right, a large panel van appeared in Rosie's mirror, sat there for about a minute, then pulled out to overtake.

'Oh, you stupid little man,' Rosie said, without much rancour. 'If it was possible to go faster on this road, don't you think I'd be doing it?' She edged the Korean tank towards the nearside verge.

It was a good enough road with no on-coming traffic so there was no reason for what happened next. The van drew level, began to pull ahead, then without warning lunged into Rosie's path, slamming her front wing with all its weight. Designed to shrug off the occasional collision with an ox, the car was nevertheless

151

shaken to its suspension; it ricocheted between the verge and the van, still unaccountably holding its position, before Rosie, wide-eyed and open-mouthed, could bring it under control. 'What the *hell*—?'

The van had veered away for a moment, but only to swing back with renewed violence. The second impact tore the wheel from Rosie's hands: the car swerved wildly, the big tyres lost their grip, and when they broadsided the edge of the road the Korean tank turned over.

It actually flew, turning about its axis as it did, further than the width of the verge. Beyond that was a grassy slope, and below that a bend of the river. The 4x4 landed on its roof and skidded downhill in a welter of flying debris and the scream of tortured steel which did not abate until it came to rest upside down in the shingle shallows.

CHAPTER ELEVEN

Matt Gosling had not only chosen a top-floor office, he'd bought a top-floor flat. At least there was a decent lift here when he moved in, but inside there were changes of level between almost every room and the next. The building was commissioned in the 1880s as offices for an insurance company; in the 1980s they moved into a steel-and-glass tower overlooking the Birmingham Bull Ring and the Skipley offices were converted into flats. Matt's was described as the Penthouse. An equally accurate label would have been the attics.

They were in his bedroom, at the top of a flight of five steps. A man with two good feet would hardly have noticed them except as a design feature; but when Matt first came here, not long enough out of hospital, there were nights when they were the last straw and he slept on the sitting-room couch.

He was out of breath now, if for a different reason. 'Alex,' he panted, 'I hope I'm not taking advantage of you.'

Alex, too, had been exerting herself, enough to produce a fine dew across her brow. She did not, of course, sweat so much as glow and her breathing was barely elevated. 'Of course not. I'm enjoying myself.'

He shook his head in wonder, droplets of perspiration falling like tiny tears from his eyelashes. 'If you knew how I agonized about asking you!'

She favoured him with a little smile he could almost swear was affectionate. 'That was silly. I owed you a favour for helping with Rosie. Anyway, I wanted to see your flat. It has tons of potential. Now.' She patted his hand condescendingly. 'Let's get this finished, shall we? Push. No, harder than that! Put a bit of muscle into it. That's better. Nearly there. One more good shove'll do it.'

When the bureau was in place under the

bedroom window they stood back, mopping their faces, to admire their handiwork. 'It's a big improvement,' Alex decided. 'That window needed something substantial to anchor it, tie it in. And the bureau looks better with the things you have in here than it did in the sitting-room. Happier.'

Matt could only nod agreement. Personally, he didn't give a toss how happy his bureau was as long as it held his papers and didn't trap his fingers in its drop-front. But if Alex said it should be in here, it was worth the effort of moving it to have her help.

'Now,' she said, turning on one heel to survey the room, 'what about that chest in the hall?'

Matt was saved from contemplating his chest's felicity by the ringing of the telephone. He picked up the receiver by the bed. 'Gosling.'

It was Rosie, calling from Edinburgh Royal Infirmary. But distance alone didn't account for the hollowness in her voice. 'Rosie, what's happened? Are you all right?'

'More or less,' she said. 'We've been in an accident. I'll give you the full SP later but right now there isn't much time. I need you to meet Shad and Fee off the Edinburgh train, Birmingham New Street, about ten fifteen. I don't want them going home tonight. Will you take them to an hotel? You'll have to pay, I don't expect either of them has much money.'

'No problem. But Rosie, what are you
154

saying? That they're in danger? What's going on?'

'Matt, I honestly don't know. Possibly nothing. What happened to us could have been sheer bad luck. We were run off the road by a van. Maybe it was just a drunk driver, I don't know. But if it was deliberate it was because of the questions we've been asking, and the man we've been asking them of knows where Fee lives and that she'll be there tonight.'

'I'm on my way,' said Matt. 'But I hope I can pick them out of a crowd on a railway station. Can you describe them?'

'Alex has met Fee. Get her to go with you.'

Matt's cheeks flushed crimson and he stammered, 'What ... how ... how did you know?'

Rosie's laugh, tired as well as dirty, reverberated in the wires. 'I didn't. I meant, you could pick her up. I gather there's no need. Gee, given a little encouragement you really get stuck in there, don't you?' He was still spluttering denials when she put down the phone.

There was no time to waste. Matt explained to Alex in the car.

'Run off the road?' she exclaimed in horror. 'Was she hurt?'

'More shocked, I think. But she's afraid that if it was deliberate there could be someone waiting for the girl at home. Hell, Alex, doesn't that sound a bit, well ... paranoid? Someone's

155

going to travel from Edinburgh to give her some grief?'

Alex stared at him. 'Someone who's prepared to crash a car with two people in it isn't going to draw the line at a few hours' journey! Matt, if it wasn't an accident this has got seriously nasty. Never mind the hotel, I'll take Fee home with me. Can you put the boy up?'

'Sure,' shrugged Matt. 'Is somebody after him, too?'

Alex breathed impatiently at him. 'Rosie wouldn't have asked for our help if she hadn't been worried. Let's do her the courtesy of assuming she has a reason and keep them out of harm's way, at least till we talk to her again.'

Matt said nothing. When he'd hoped for company this evening a psychic gardener wasn't what he had had in mind.

They took Alex's car because they needed room for four. They just had time to park before the train pulled in and began disgorging passengers. Waiting by the gate they scanned the passing faces, afraid they'd slip by unnoticed in the crowd.

In the event, though, they spotted them easily enough, Shad's dark curly head bent over Fee's cropped fair one as he steered her towards the exit. The girl looked exhausted, Alex thought; in fact they both did. As they neared the barrier she raised her hand and waved. 'Fee, Shad—over here.'

156

She made no effort to explain there and then. 'Rosie called me. Come on, we've got a car outside.'

While Alex threaded the city traffic Shad recounted what had happened in Edinburgh up until their leaving and Matt told them what had happened since. The news hit Shad like a blow, his eyes recoiling. It hit Fee like a wave, threatening to swamp her. She moaned, 'Oh God,' and her eyes closed in despair.

'How are they?' Shad's voice was thin.

Matt shrugged. 'I thought maybe you could tell us.'

Alex heard the breath catch in the boy's throat. 'Are you blaming me for this?'

'Of course not,' she intervened quickly. Little more was said during the rest of the short drive to Skipley.

Numb with horror, Fee raised no argument to what was proposed, but after they'd dropped the women at Alex's flat Shad told Matt he was going home. 'Even if Rosie's right I can't be in any danger. Nobody knows where I live.'

'Are you sure about that?'

'Yeah. Fee left her address so they could pass on any news, but nobody even knows my name.'

'What about the police?'

'Well, yes.' He scowled. 'You don't really think Edinburgh police are going to be lying in wait for me?'

Matt shook his head. 'No. But you forgot

about them so maybe you've forgotten someone else.'

But Shad was too tired to argue, too tired for anything but stubborn insistence. 'I'm going home. If you won't drive me I'll walk.'

'Fine,' said Matt irritably. 'High Street, was it? Which end?'

Thursdays were less hectic than Wednesdays but together they left him shattered. Usually he went straight home and put his feet up, but when a casual conversation with Alex in the lift took a promising turn suddenly he felt much fresher. But that was seven hours, some furniture removals, a worrying phone call and a round-trip to Birmingham ago, and now he was running on empty. He had cramp in the foot he hadn't got.

'Hang on,' said Shad, remembering, 'can you take me to Foxford instead? I left my car at Prufrock's and I'll need it in the morning.'

The piebald Land Rover was where he'd left it. Even were sleepy Foxford a hotbed of motor crime, only someone who'd already purloined a trailer full of sheep would have stolen it. A ten-year-old Skoda with go-faster stripes had more cachet.

As the car drew up in Foxford Lane Shad was already halfway out. Then he looked back over his shoulder, his face creased and awkward. 'Thanks for the lift.'

'You're welcome,' Matt said insincerely, waiting for him to close the door. He knew he

158

was behaving badly but didn't care. He was annoyed about his evening, worried about Rosie, and disappointed in Shad Lucas. He knew that was unreasonable. The ·boy was a gardener: Matt had no right to expect him to be interesting or charismatic or anything else. He appeared to have an unusual talent. Matt had known a number of gifted men, had never met one who was as good company as the shiftless idlers you found in every mess whose only talent was to amuse. Charm was the favourite strategy of the feckless. Still Matt felt oddly cheated that the most improbable character to come his way since Rosie Holland should prove so comprehensively dull.

Shad nodded quickly; hidden by the night his cheeks flamed. He had no illusions about how he seemed to these intelligent, successful people. He wasn't a stupid man but they made him feel stupid—slow, awkward and cloddish. But for a fluke of nature the only way he'd have known any of them was knocking the mud off his boots once a week to collect his wages at their back doors. That was fine, he was doing for money something they hadn't the skill, energy or time to do for themselves. But forced into their company without even a begonia for moral support he was out of his depth.

When Prufrock made some joke he didn't understand, and Fee smiled and Rosie guffawed, he felt like a changeling left on the doorstep. He listened to them talk casually, not

159

thinking they were being clever, not meaning to display their erudition, and was acutely aware he was piss-poor company by comparison. He lacked both native charm and acquired polish. He'd sat opposite Fee Morris, on whom he ached to make an impression, for five hours and hadn't made one witty or otherwise memorable remark.

So he wanted to be on his way as much as Matt wanted to be rid of him. But he felt, obscurely but pressingly, that he had something to apologize for. He wasn't sure what, only that somehow he'd let them down. He said gruffly, 'When you know more ... about Rosie and Arthur ...'

Matt nodded. 'Leave me your number, I'll call you.'

Shad gritted his teeth. 'I don't have a phone. If I call your office tomorrow—?'

'Fine. If I'm not there ask for the editor, Dan Sale. He'll know whatever there is to know.'

On that they parted, Shad hurrying to the Land Rover as if it were raining and driving off without a backward look.

Matt sat in the parked car a minute longer, reflecting on the evening's events and feeling, as Shad had, to have acquitted himself without much distinction. He was a generous man; he didn't treat the office gopher that brusquely. He'd commanded soldiers you could only consider secret weapons for the other side, and treated them with less disdain. He didn't know

160

why he resented a man whose only crime was wanting to sleep in his own bed. He vented a little exasperated sigh and went to drive off.

Which was when he glimpsed movement inside the cottage.

A civilian might have thought he was mistaken. It was late, the row was in darkness—perhaps a little summer zephyr had twitched the curtain at the downstairs window. But a soldier's life can depend on his judgement, on distinguishing between little sounds and movements that mean nothing and others that might be the only warning he'll get of an enemy presence; and though he only glimpsed it from the corner of his eye Matt had no doubt what he'd seen. Someone in the room had passed the window.

He didn't stop the car. He drove up the lane, turned the corner and stopped there, out of sight, while he thought.

He could have been looking at the wrong cottage. But he knew he wasn't. Shad had given him the number, and he checked as he drove off. Prufrock could have had someone staying with him, but Rosie had been to the cottage twice without seeing anyone. Also, this was what Rosie had been afraid of, why she'd wanted him to meet the train. She thought someone could be waiting for one or other of them. Matt got out of the car, taking a torch from the glove compartment.

He'd been a soldier too recently to return up

161

the lane. Instead he looked for the back alley that common sense told him a terrace of cottages must have. It was rough and unlit, and he didn't dare use the torch, but as his eyes adjusted to the night he moved with growing confidence, counting off the cottages until he came to Prufrock's. The topiary hedges gave him a momentary jolt: he thought they were people waiting to jump at him. He gave a terse little grin and let himself in silently at the gate.

The back of the house was dark, too, but the kitchen door was unlocked, and Matt didn't believe Prufrock would have left it that way. There was still an outside chance that the old man had some clandestine company: if so they'd both have to accept his good intentions and apologies. Summoning the police would only make things worse if Mr Chips had acquired a live-in bimbette.

As he entered the house Matt was conscious of his heart thumping and the tension of his muscles, aware of the old adrenalin high that got you into, and out of, situations where you'd no business being. He didn't know whose shadow had crossed the window, but if it wasn't bad news from Edinburgh some burglar was about to get the shock of his life being jumped by six foot two and thirteen stone of fully trained if currently sub-standard Paratrooper.

Last time he did this for real it was the IRA waiting for him, and he doubted Edinburgh could match that. Of course, last time he'd also had a loaded gun in his hand, a trained platoon at his back, and enough feet to leg it if things went wrong.

Stealth was his best weapon now. He knew no one could have heard him. He crossed the kitchen, feeling his way with the backs of his fingers, and listened at the door before edging it open. He allowed himself a moment's pleasure at how much of the old skill remained.

At the end of the tiny hall was the front door, to his left the stairs, to his right the living room. The door was shut. He listened again, laid his hand on it lightly, testing for resistance. There was none: it opened with a murmur.

There wasn't much light in the room— Foxford Lane had only two dim yellow streetlights, neither of them directly outside— but after the blackness in the hall there was enough for Matt to be sure the room was empty. He straightened, exhaling slowly. Had he been mistaken? Had it indeed been a burglar, who'd finished and gone while Matt was tip-toeing up the back alley? He ran the torch round the room and it almost looked as if it had been burgled, not ransacked exactly, but someone had emptied drawers on to the table as if looking for something.

There was still upstairs. The movement he'd seen was down here, and he didn't believe that he'd given enough warning of his approach to send the intruder scurrying aloft. But he might have been waiting long enough to need a leak, and it had been hammered into Matt often enough that the building wasn't secure until all the building was secure. He returned to the hall. Stairs again: he gave a quick, un-self-pitying grin. Who'd have thought the world had so many stairs in it? He kept the torch low, just in case.

He had no intimation of danger. He thought whoever had been here had gone. The last thing he expected was to reach the top of the stairs and be hit in the ribs by a pick-axe handle swung with devastating force by someone hidden round the angle of the landing.

The impact drove the air out of his lungs in a startled grunt. There wasn't time for any more—not fear, not pain, not anger. The blow would have floored him on level ground, at the top of the stairs it launched him into space. He was halfway down before he landed, crashing on his hip on the edge of a tread thinly padded by carpet. The torch had gone flying. His flailing hands found the rail, his head cannoned off the woodwork, and the world turned over and slid out of focus.

He didn't quite lose consciousness. He was aware of a hand in his collar trailing him to the foot of the stairs, of an oddly unconcerned awareness of pain as his bruises acquired bruises, of a figure in the darkness sitting him up against the wall and playing torchlight in his eyes. He groaned and swatted feebly at the beam. Like a mosquito it danced away from his

164

hand and travelled down his legs. Even in his befuddled state Matt realized it was lingering longer than it should, and he made the effort to look where it was pointing. Then he understood his assailant's preoccupation with his feet. One of them had come off.

On better form Matt could have used the advantage of surprise to regain the initiative. He thought he was the bigger man; he probably knew more about the science of fighting. If he could grapple the other to the floor he could take that stave off him and make him wish he'd kept his day job. But he was still dizzy, couldn't have stood up even if he hadn't left one foot halfway up the stairs; a child could have bested him now. And this wasn't a child. Nor was it a burglar: a burglar might have knocked him down with a pick-axe handle but wouldn't have spent this long looking at him. He'd have either fled or beaten Matt's brains in by now.

Finally he spoke; just one word, but the accent was enough to confirm that it wasn't a local burglar. 'Who?'

So he knows I'm not Prufrock, thought Matt. He thinks I might be Shad. And what he does next depends on that. 'I'm from next door. I heard something. I've called the police,' he lied hopefully.

'No,' said the man; and Matt had to admit it wasn't very likely. A watchful neighbour hearing movement in a house that should be empty might investigate or he might call the police: he wouldn't do both.

But there was nothing to lose by making the intruder wonder. 'They'll be here any minute.' If nothing else, while they were talking they weren't fighting and Matt's senses were trickling back. Any minute now he'd have a crack at that stick.

It was a very small hall: the sound of a key turning in the front door sent a shockwave through both of them. It wasn't the police, Matt knew that; part of his brain not wholly concerned with surviving the next five minutes knew who it was; but mostly it was a distraction to the man standing over him. There mightn't be another chance. As the door swung in and the intruder's eyes followed it, Matt dived for his legs.

Shad came in on a tangle of limbs and a volley of imprecations, half of which he didn't understand. In that moment he had no idea that two of the arms and one of the legs belonged to Matt: he found a fight in progress in what should have been an empty house, saw a pick-axe handle in the middle of it, grabbed it and flung it down the garden. Whatever was going on, that was out of order. He groped for the light in the hopes of making sense of this writhing, grunting, sweating, swearing tangle of humanity.

As he fumbled for the switch one of the protagonists broke out of the mêlée, shouldered him aside and was doing the four-minute mile down the garden path before the light came on. Shad thought of giving chase but doubted he could make up the lost ground. Instead he turned his attention to the remaining intruder. He stared. 'Matt?'

It's hard to look nonchalant when you've been knocked downstairs with a pick-axe handle, had your head bounced off the banister and been detached from one of your extremities, but Matt tried. 'Shad. What are you doing back here?'

Shad's voice soared. 'What am *I* doing here? What are *you* doing here? How did you get in?'

'The back door was open. I saw movement in here, crept round the back, found the door unlocked. When I went to look upstairs I got jumped. I imagine this is what Rosie warned us about, only the sod was waiting for you here instead of at home.'

'For me?' That knocked the wind out of him.

Matt shrugged. 'He can't have been expecting me, and Prufrock's with Rosie. Either he knew you'd come for the Land Rover, or he was searching Prufrock's papers for your address.'

The dark eyes flared in alarm. 'Fee? Alex?'

Matt shook his head. 'There's no way he could know who Alex is or where she lives. But it's as well Fee didn't go home tonight. Er . . . do me a favour, will you? Pass me my foot.'

While he was reattaching it he tried again to discover why Shad had returned. 'You must have been halfway home. What made you come back?'

'I don't know,' admitted Shad. 'I heard something.'

'From over The Brink? Ah. You mean . . .?'

Shad wasn't sure if it would be ruder to watch what Matt was doing or to look away. He stared at his own feet. 'I suppose. I don't know. I didn't know till just now that I wasn't imagining it.'

'That's better.' Matt stood up, keeping one hand on the wall. 'My head's still swimming. I'll call the police. You'll have to stay till they've been. I'll let Alex know what's going on. Christ, what a mess!' Thinking of Alex reminded him. 'Shit. I never locked her car. All I need now is for somebody to nick that!'

Shad held out his hand for the keys. 'I'll do it. Where did you leave it?' Matt told him.

Matt must have been ten minutes on the phone with the police, most of that time convincing them he wasn't making this up. When they realized he was in earnest they told him to stay where he was, they were on their way.

He changed his mind about calling Alex. It was late, she was probably asleep by now, and he really didn't see how she could be in danger. First thing in the morning would be time enough. Surely to God nothing else would happen before that?

Just about then it struck him Shad was

168

taking his time. A momentary discomfort shivered up his spine and he went to the window. There was nothing to see so he walked as far as the gate. The car was out of sight but there was something by the corner, at the very limit of the streetlamp's glow—not Shad returning but something dropped in the road. Maybe a coat? Maybe the running man had dropped his coat; maybe—miracles do happen occasionally—he'd left his wallet in the pocket.

So why hadn't Shad picked it up by now?

Fear plucked at his heart. His swimming head and battered body forgotten, he began walking up the quiet lane. After a moment he contrived a broken run.

It wasn't a coat lying in the road. It was Shad Lucas spilled like rubbish in the gutter, face down, quite still. He didn't respond when Matt gasped his name nor to the touch of his hand; and when Matt carefully lifted his head he saw why. He'd been shot in the face. His blood was pooled in the dusty roadway under him.

CHAPTER TWELVE

Matt was still in shock when Alex found him bent over a table with three plastic cups of scummy hospital coffee on it. He wasn't drinking the stuff; he was just buying it and watching it go cold. Alex had never seen him look so ill. She dropped into a chair beside him, catching his hand. 'Oh, Matt. What about you? Are you all right?'

He'd started at her touch and the eyes he raised to her were haggard. But he'd never been so glad to see anyone in his life. 'God, Alex—what the hell are we involved in here?'

Even the police hadn't been able to tell him that; they both knew he wasn't expecting an answer from Alex. She shook her head. 'Were you hurt?'

'A bit of concussion, maybe a cracked rib,' he said dully. 'Nothing much. Not beside—' He jerked his head at the door where hospital staff were coming and going.

Alex held his shaking hand tight. 'Is there any news? What do they say?'

'It's an hour since they took him into surgery. They haven't said anything. But, oh Christ, Alex, that bastard shot him in the face! The bullet's in his brain. Even if they pull him through, what's going to be left? Maybe it's better if he dies. Maybe he'd want to die.'

'Don't say that,' she said sharply. 'The only thing we know for sure about brain injuries is that we know nothing for sure. People die of bumping their heads on shelves, and survive losing a quarter of their brain tissue. Two people come into hospital with identical injuries, and one never regains consciousness and the other's back at work in three months. Shad is young, he's strong—there's every reason to hope he'll make a good recovery.'

170

But Matt had cradled him in the road while Prufrock's neighbours, roused by his parade-ground bellows as they had not been by the sound of the shot, called an ambulance and ran for blankets and made hot sweet tea, and an awareness of the frailty of life had entered his soul. Life was a toy balloon tethered by a thread, and if that thread broke it made no difference that the body it left behind was young and fit and sturdy: only the pathologist would even notice. What mattered was the thread, and that anchoring the spirit of Shad Lucas to his strong, terribly still young body was drawn as thin as gossamer.

'It was my fault.' His voice was low and thin: not the strapping of his ribs but grief and guilt like steel bands round his chest kept his breathing shallow. 'If I'd locked the goddamned car . . .!'

'That's silly,' Alex chided him. 'You may as well say it's Rosie's fault for involving him, or Fee's for involving any of us. We're none of us to blame. Whoever pointed a gun in his face and pulled the trigger, that's who's responsible.'

'Where is Fee?' asked Matt, finally missing her and looking round.

'I didn't bring her. To be honest,' admitted Alex, 'I didn't tell her. I left a note saying there was a problem at the office and I'd had to go in. There seemed no point waking her. There's nothing she could do here. You and I can fret

171

enough for all of us, and she's safer where she is.' She bit her lip. 'There is someone we should inform. Shad's mother. God knows how we're going to find her. All I know is she works at the end of a pier.'

'The police'll find her address at his flat.' He looked round vaguely, uncertain how to proceed.

Alex patted his hand. 'You stay here. I'll see to it.'

She hadn't far to look. Detective Superintendent Marsh was talking to the casualty registrar, trying to get some kind of a prognosis. Dr Ashwar used longer words than Alex but basically she was saying the same thing: that they didn't know if Shad Lucas would live, nor would they until either his brain stem activity ceased or he was sitting up complaining about the food. 'That's the best guide. People who don't notice how bad the food is should still be in ICU.'

Alex introduced herself. The registrar looked wry at being caught out in a moment of levity, but, though she could have been more tactful there was nothing she could add. 'We'll have a better idea when we see how he coped with the surgery, but it could be days before we can say with any confidence.'

Alex told Marsh the little she knew about Shad's mother. He nodded. 'I'll get someone round to his flat, see what we can find out.'

Dr Ashwar was pursing her lips. 'Forgive me,

but can I ask you to treat that as urgent? We need to speak to Mrs Lucas as soon as possible.'

Alex felt her heart turn over and sink. 'You mean, if she wants to see him alive . . .?'

'Yes, that too. But if he's going to die he'll do it whether or not his mother's here, and in some ways it's easier for relatives if it's already over. No, I meant . . .' She took a deep breath. 'Miss Fisher, understand that as long as there is any chance of saving your friend, that is our only concern. But if we can't do that, if our best efforts just aren't equal to the task, then we have another duty. Do you know—has he ever discussed with you—his feelings about organ donation?'

It shouldn't have been a surprise, not when the doctor had been so honest about Shad's condition, but the implications hit Alex under the heart. They were already thinking of him in terms of a crop to be harvested. 'I'm sorry,' she stammered. 'I haven't known him very long. I just don't know him that well.'

'I'm sorry to have to raise it while everyone's still in shock,' said the registrar. 'But if we can't save him, then every minute counts. If we knew it was something he'd want to do he'd be a gift to the donor programme—a fit, healthy young man with nothing damaged but his brain. Heart, lungs, kidneys, liver, cornea: he could bequeath new life to six or seven people. But we need the permission of his next-of-kin, and

173

I presume that would be his mother.'

Marsh nodded sombrely. It wasn't the first time such considerations had cut across an inquiry, and he recognized that accommodating them was almost as important as finding out who stood face to face with this young man and put a bullet in his brain. But it was one of those moments when he was infinitely glad to be the plodding policeman with his boring suit and his boring questions, and not the glamorous doctor in the white coat. There might be times in the days ahead when what he had to say would cause that same flicker of horror in this woman's eyes, but she'd forgive him because she knew he was doing his best for her friend. He was profoundly glad he didn't have to tell her that, if it wasn't good enough, he'd quite like to carve him up. 'I'll get on to it.'

Alex nodded. 'You'd better call Edinburgh police as well. Shad was just off the train, and the people he was with there have been attacked, too.'

The policeman's eyes widened; obviously he'd have liked to ask her more. But he was conscious of Dr Ashwar's anxiety and anyway he'd probably get a clearer story from his Edinburgh colleagues. 'I'll need to talk to you later.'

'I'll be here.'

She went back to Matt. He'd bought some more coffee. When she took a cup and drank it

174

he looked at her in surprise, as if she'd come up with a whole new use for it.

By the time Detective Superintendent Marsh in Skipley had talked to Detective Sergeant Rush in Edinburgh, both men were deeply confused. They now had to treat this tale of ornithologists, postcards and psychic gardeners as more than a fever-dream, even if they couldn't imagine what it all meant. These strange people, whose association with a newspaper was not lost on the policemen, could have dreamt up much of what they said but nothing altered the fact that three of them were in hospital, one at least the victim of a murder attempt. That was the bottom line. Whatever was going on was real enough and important enough to someone to justify that ultimate sanction.

'You'll tell them, will you?' Marsh finished. 'Holland and Prufrock—you'll tell them what's happened this end?'

'I will,' promised DS Rush. 'If they say they're heading back, should I try and stop them?'

'From what I'm told of Ms Holland, I think you may save your breath. Anyway, if it's open season on them at both ends they'd better decide where they want to be. At least nobody'll blame us if the worst happens.'

'Want to bet?' muttered Rush morosely.

Marsh questioned Matt again, but there was nothing he could add to his first statement. The events were clear enough in his mind. He found an intruder in Prufrock's house and fought with him. When Shad returned the man ran off; when he went outside the man was waiting with a gun.

'What did he say? In the house, when you confronted him?'

'Hardly anything. He wanted to know who I was. And he didn't believe me when I said I'd called the police.'

'And you've no idea who it was? Could it have been someone you'd met before?'

'Superintendent, it could have been my old CO! I never got a clear look at him. He only said a couple of words and by then I'd already been knocked downstairs. Don't waste your time putting together an identity parade, I couldn't pick him out if the others were Laurel and Hardy and The Three Stooges. Except—' He stopped then, frowning, thinking.

'Except?'

'I think he was foreign. There was a definite accent, and he sort of fired the words at me. He said, "Who?"—barked it, rather—when anyone I know would have said, "Who're you?" however much of a hurry they were in. Also, he wasn't swearing in English.'

'Any idea where he was from?'

Matt could only shake his head. 'Sorry.'

Alex went back to the news from Edinburgh. 'Rosie and Prufrock are all right? I mean, give or take a scratch or two?'

Marsh nodded. 'They're fine. The old man's got his arm in a sling, Ms Holland needed a couple of stitches in her forehead, that's all. Rush said, looking at the car he couldn't imagine how they'd walked away. The bodywork must have absorbed the impact. She can say goodbye to her no claims bonus, though.'

Left alone, Matt and Alex sat a long time in silence. There were things they'd have to do soon—tell Fee, tell Dan, get through to Rosie—but two o'clock in the morning wasn't the time for any of them. They sat and waited. At one point Matt lapsed into an exhausted slumber. Alex made sure no one disturbed him until the surgeon came.

He was a small man in his thirties, with delicate musician's hands. He wiped perspiration off one eyebrow with the side of his thumb. 'OK, this is the situation. The bullet hit him just below the left eye on a rising angle and punched through to the under-surface of the brain at the junction of the anterior and middle lobes. This is, of course, a serious injury.

'But it could have been worse. Small calibre bullets cause less destruction than big ones. It missed all the vital structures behind his eye: as far as I can see there should be no permanent damage to his vision. And it didn't bounce around—it came out cleanly the way it went in, which means the injury wasn't made worse by anything we had to do.

'I can't promise that he'll recover but I'm happier about his chances now than when they wheeled him in. We've tidied him up, stopped the bleeding, and I didn't see anything in there that said we were in deep shit. His vital signs are as good as can be expected, he should start regaining consciousness when we cut back on the sedation. We'll need to keep him under for a while—the best thing we can do for the swelling you get with any brain injury is keep the patient still.'

The surgeon stretched weary muscles in his shoulders as if he'd just finished a shift at the coalface. 'What I can't yet tell you is how he's been affected by this. Our brains govern everything we are and do in incredibly complex ways. Destroyed tissue won't regenerate but that doesn't mean that all function lost is lost for ever. The undamaged areas try to compensate, seek other ways to achieve the same end. Sometimes they're successful, sometimes not. It's notoriously difficult to predict at this stage who's going to leave in a wheelchair and who's going to run for a bus.

'I'm saying all this because I don't want you to be alarmed when he first wakes up. If he gets that far I'd expect him to continue making progress, though it'll certainly take weeks, probably months, conceivably years. What we can't predict is how much progress he's capable of. That, only time will tell.' He half turned,

178

then looked back. 'If either of you goes in for praying, now would be a good time.'

*   *   *

Arthur Prufrock woke to the sound of a car, and for a minute couldn't remember where he was. Certainly not at home: with so many bird pictures that was like waking in an aviary. And not the hospital. He remembered being in the hospital. He remembered the crash, the car turning over, the straps of his seatbelt digging into him. Then it stopped, down on the river's edge, and he was hanging from the straps and so was Rosie Holland at his side, breathing like a bellows, blood in her hair from a cut on her forehead.

Shock kept them hanging there when they should have been getting out. At length Rosie turned her head, her eyes stretched, her voice unsteady. 'Are you all right?'

Prufrock nodded; upside down, the effect wasn't what he expected. 'Yes.' His voice was gruff.

'How do we get out?'

Prufrock considered. Surrounded by the teenage boys who were the perfect audience he'd seen all the James Bond films: he knew what happened when cars went off cliffs. You got a minute's respite, just enough to start breathing again, then . . . 'Quickly, and carefully; and me first so I can give you a hand.'

That was how he sprained his wrist: breaking his fall when he released his seatbelt. Then he freed Rosie, helping her through the door that now opened at an unfamiliar angle.

The car didn't explode or catch fire. It just sat there looking mournful until they turned their backs on it and trudged up to the road. The first two cars that came along ignored them; the third stopped when Rosie stood in its path. An hour later they were back in Edinburgh, being strapped and stitched, and explaining what had happened to an incredulous Detective Sergeant Rush.

At about midnight they returned to Mrs Mackey's house in Cowgate. Her first instinct, before she saw the state they were in, was to borrow some dogs to set on them; but seeing it was a genuine crisis she rose to it and made them a hot supper before sending them to bed. Which is where Prufrock woke: in the guest room in the top of Mrs Mackey's tall old house.

He sat on the edge of the bed in his underwear for a minute, testing his body for creaks. There were more this morning than last night but he still thought they'd got off lightly. His watch read six forty—early enough to retreat under the covers, but he didn't think he'd sleep if he did. He thought moving round would do him more good. He dressed carefully, settled his arm in its sling and went to see if Rosie was astir.

There was no answer to his tap at her door.

He should have gone away and tried later—it was, after all, a lady's bedroom. But that was no lady, that was the person he was in a car crash with last night. He opened the door a diffident inch.

Rosie was both awake and up. At first Prufrock thought she was applying make-up, which surprised him a little: for all the good it did, why bother? But though hunched over the dressing table she wasn't wrestling with powder and lipstick. Her back was to him and he saw her broad shoulders shudder. She was crying, and trying to do it softly for fear of disturbing people.

'Rosie, whatever's the matter?' He came forward, tried to fold her in his good arm. 'Is it last night? It's all right, it's only shock—it catches up on you afterwards. It was a horrid thing to happen but it could have been worse. Your poor old car took a beating but at least we're all right.'

'Stuff the car,' she sobbed. 'Oh, God, Arthur, I don't know how to tell you. Detective Sergeant Rush was here. Skipley police called him. It's Shad. There was someone in your house when he went for his Land Rover; he and Matt tackled him and Shad was shot. In the face. He's been in surgery half the night. They're still not sure if he's going to live.'

All the strength went out of Prufrock's legs and he sat down abruptly on the bed. 'Oh. Oh, no,' he moaned. 'Oh, dear God. Why? *Why?*'

'Because I dragged him into this against all his better instincts,' Rosie retorted bitterly, raising a face streaked with tears. 'Because Auntie Rosie knows best—always, no matter what the subject, no matter who stands to get hurt. Arthur, the first time he looked at me he was afraid. I saw it in his eyes. He was afraid of me. He knew then I was going to get him killed. That's why he didn't want to come, only we gave him no choice.'

Her voice was running up towards an angry hysteria. Prufrock was stunned, too, but he forced himself to stay calm. They used to say at the Argyll Academical Institution that if the Russians nuked Glasgow the first thing you'd hear after the flash would be Prudence Prufrock saying in clipped and measured tones, 'Keep your heads, boys, there's no need to panic.'

'That's silly talk and it doesn't get us anywhere,' he said sternly. He didn't quite get it out without a quiver but he doubted Rosie would notice. 'Shad came for the same reason you and I did: because he wanted to help. When you've known him a bit longer you'll know he can't be made to do anything he doesn't want to. He's obstinate and pig-headed, and right now those are the two best things going for him. Shad Lucas isn't going to die—not now, not from this. He's too damn stubborn to.'

There was some truth in that. There are

182

injuries that no one survives, but there's also a huge grey area where the potential for recovery can be aided or hindered by mental attitude. In such circumstances a degree of bloody-mindedness can be a real asset.

'So,' said Prufrock, standing up. 'We'd better find out when there's a train.'

Rosie nodded shakily. 'Yes, of course, you'll want to be there. I'm sorry I can't give you a lift to the station. That's about the first thing I'd better do—get hold of a car.'

In Prufrock's ice-blue eyes the concern was sharpening to alarm. 'You're not thinking of staying? Rosie, you can't. Somebody tried to kill you here yesterday!'

'Someone damn near killed Shad at home. Whoever these people are, whatever they're up to, it's more than a little local difficulty we can get away from on a train. You'll want to be with Shad, I understand that. But I have things to do here.'

He made one last attempt, sure as he did so that he was wasting his breath. 'Shall I have a word with Sergeant Rush? I'm sure he won't need you to stay. We both gave statements last night. He can phone us if he needs anything else, and we can come back if he gets as far as arresting someone. He won't expect us to stay for the duration of his inquiry.'

'No, he said that.' Rosie's voice hardened. 'That's not why I'm staying. Malcolm Jamison is behind what happened to Philip Morris, what

183

happened to us, and what's happened to Shad. I'll leave when I've seen him nailed to the wall and not before.'

Defeated, Prufrock sighed. 'I see. Well, I can't leave you here alone. We'll have to impose on Mrs Mackey a little longer.'

When Rosie smiled there was a warmth there that made people ashamed all they'd noticed before was the agrarian substance and functionality of her features. 'I wasn't going to ask. But Jesus Christ, Arthur, I'd have hated to see you go.'

Prufrock filtered a chuckle through the little toothbrush moustache. 'Why, Miss Holland, I haven't had a woman say that to me for years.' Then, moved to match her honesty with his own, he added wryly, 'Well, ever, actually.'

CHAPTER THIRTEEN

Their first call, as soon as Edinburgh was awake, was a secondhand car dealer near the Union Canal. They hadn't yet discussed trying to reach Oban again, but even if they didn't— and certainly the *White Heather* would have left by now—there was no point staying if the only leads they could pursue were to areas on a good bus route.

Rosie wasn't sure what their next move should be but all her instincts told her that the answers were here, in Edinburgh, not a million miles from a little white-painted building with a flying goose over the door.

It was a police matter now. Detective Sergeant Rush knew everything Rosie knew and all she suspected. The inquiry was in his hands, unless somebody more senior had already taken over, and he would not be amused if in her grief and rage she sprang traps he was carefully setting for the sleek Mr Jamison. Before she indulged her desire to bounce him off the walls she'd need to think the implications through, maybe talk to Rush again.

He would try to dissuade her, probably try to send her home. He wouldn't succeed. This started off as Fee's trouble, with Rosie trying to help because solving other people's problems was her job. But what had been business this time yesterday was personal now. It wasn't in her to back down from confrontation. She was not immune to threats, had examined too many broken bodies to retain any illusions about her own mortality. Still she couldn't abide being pushed around. It wasn't that her drive for self-preservation was undeveloped, more that, however fast it cut in, her temper cut in faster.

So it was the car dealer first, Detective Sergeant Rush second and—unless the policeman came up with some persuasive arguments—Malcolm Jamison after that.

She didn't want a replacement for the Korean tank. She would make a permanent choice at her leisure, and buy it close to home so she could go and make a scene whenever something went wrong. What she wanted now was something cheap enough to buy on her chequebook, big enough that she could get behind the wheel, and sturdy enough to take a little punishment. After seeing what a moderate crash had done to a car built like a Stalinist ballbearing factory she didn't want to risk her skin in anything flimsy. She settled on a ten-year-old black Volvo estate that felt solid, sounded lusty, and looked like a hearse.

'It's . . . sober,' allowed Prufrock.

'If we put down the back seat, you could lie in state with a lily on your chest and upset people in traffic jams.'

He nodded. 'Then again, I could not.'

Rush wasn't at the police station and Rosie declined the offered substitute. 'I'll catch up with him later.'

She phoned the *Chronicle*. By Friday the mayhem was over so Dan Sale was at his desk, checking the issue for blunders he'd spend all next week fielding. He remembered with horror a series of typographical errors compounded by cack-handed attempts to correct them that resulted in the paper marrying a bride to her own father. It had taken abject apologies to sort out and Dan hated carrying corrections, took each one as an attack on his competence.

But the worst he'd found by the time Rosie

186

phoned was a misplaced apostrophe suggesting that the little town of Skipley had more than one mayor, which was stupid but probably not actionable, even when set in 68-point bold across ten columns.

He'd already heard an outline of the night's events from Matt. He had Rosie confirm that she really was all right, she wasn't just saying that, and Prufrock was all right, too, before he'd answer any questions. He might have been worrying about an insurance claim but Rosie thought he was genuinely anxious about them. 'What about Shad? Is there any news from the hospital?'

'Matt called them about half an hour ago, before I sent him home to bed,' said Dan. 'There's no great change. They aren't expecting one till they're ready to bring him round. They're fairly happy with his EEG and ECG and whatever else they measure. They didn't exactly say so but we got the impression they'd be surprised if he upped and died now. The next big hurdle will be when they stop the sedation and find out how much of his brain's still functioning.' He heard himself saying that and wished he hadn't. But Rosie was a pathologist: she knew the score.

'What about Fee? Where's she now, is someone looking after her?'

'She's staying with Alex. We thought that was best. I've told Alex to stay home till further notice. Fee was pretty upset, and Alex was

187

afraid if she left her alone she'd walk out and take her chances rather than risk anyone else getting hurt.'

The girl had been close to nervous exhaustion last time Rosie saw her: since then three people trying to help her had been attacked. She would blame herself. Moreover, the sudden explosion of violence put an end to any real hope that her brother would eventually come home. No one set out to murder people searching for a man who was himself alive and well. Fee wasn't stupid: she knew she'd forced Shad into a crusade for what was already a lost cause, and she'd have his fate on her conscience always. Anyone would reel under that burden.

'Dan, if Alex is staying home, do you need me in the office? Much as I want to find out what this is all about, if you need me back there I'll come.'

She heard him suck a speculative breath through his front teeth. 'I'll be honest with you, Rosie. I'd rather you were here. The way this thing's blown up I don't like you being out on a limb up there. But I'm not going to order you back and I'm not going to pretend we can't do without you for a few days. God knows how a provincial weekly's agony aunt finds herself in such a fix, but it's your decision whether and how you pursue this matter. I'm not going to tell you what to do. Except to be as careful as you know how.'

Arthur's Seat, a volcanic crag rising eight hundred feet above the city, has a history as the place where Edinburghers go to think. Rough paths lead to the summit and there's a scenic motor-road around the rough-hewn beauty of Holyrood Park. From the top you look down on three towns: the mediaeval Old Town, the Georgian New Town and the modern suburbs spreading out beyond. You can raise your eyes to the steely expanse of the Forth Estuary, or turn on your heel for a view to the Lammermuir Hills. Surrounded by space and history, present difficulties slip into perspective.

Rosie may have thought she had found her way up here by accident but in fact it was the spirits of place drawing her, the souls of all those resolved dilemmas blowing around the windy peak like chip-papers. Although Prufrock had been here before he said nothing, left the ancient iron-boned calm to work its magic on her. He offered no suggestions of his own. He was here to support her if he could, nothing more. He'd invited himself on this jaunt, it was too late to complain that he'd got more than he'd bargained for. Rosie had, too, but if she was going to see it through he had to back her up.

Then as the car cruised slowly behind the crag he spotted something that momentarily

189

knocked the breath out of him. 'Keep driving,' he hissed. 'Go on a hundred yards, then stop.'

By then Rosie had seen it, too, and her eyes shot out on stalks. She only just had the presence of mind to look the other way as she drove past. 'Wasn't that—?'

'*Yes*,' exclaimed Prufrock, angling his wing mirror to reflect the white Range Rover that would have put up every grouse in the park. 'That was indeed Mr Malcolm Jamison; nor was he alone.'

'Who . . .?'

'Don't look,' insisted Prufrock. 'Neither of them has seen this car. There's no reason for them to take any interest in us unless they catch us taking an interest in them.'

'Then tell me who it was!' By then Rosie was probably sufficiently far ahead for the occupants of the white car to think themselves alone. She let the Volvo coast to a halt.

'Put it this way,' Prufrock said with pursed lips. 'Who wasn't in his office when you asked to see him?'

'You're kidding!' Rosie screwed round in her seat to stare at the other car but it was too far to identify the occupants. 'Are you sure? That's who it was—Jamison and Rush?'

'I may be old,' said Prufrock stiffly, 'but I can tell a cormorant from a shag at a hundred yards and I can certainly recognize two men I met only yesterday when I pass within a few feet of them.'

'But, Arthur, I know it happens all the time on the telly but that's the hell of a suggestion to make about a real police officer!'

'I'm not suggesting anything. I'm saying what I saw. There may very well be an innocent explanation.'

'Such as?'

'I can't imagine,' he said honestly.

'And you're sure it was Rush?'

'Rosie, of course I'm sure! I am not an imaginative man. I don't jump to unwarranted conclusions. If there was any doubt in my mind I would say so. I got a good look, and that's who it was.'

'Did they spot you?'

He sniffed. 'Being old has few advantages but one is that you become invisible. If I'd tapped on the window and asked for directions, neither of them would have remembered me. Now: what can those two be discussing? Not at the police station and not in Jamison's office but here, where they might reasonably expect to go unnoticed.'

'It doesn't sound like a man helping the police with their inquiries, does it?' Rosie had known a lot of policemen in her previous incarnation, had found them a division of humanity with as many flaws and frailties, time-servers and heroes, bores, wits and vindictive bastards as any other. But she hadn't known any who were crooks. She could have believed half of them were fiddling their income tax and the rest claiming overtime they hadn't worked, but that was only human. This was something else. This was helping a man who took other people's lives, and she could only think of one reason a policeman would do such a thing.

'More like bribery and corruption,' agreed Prufrock. 'Which explains someone being in my house. Jamison had Fiona's address, and knew who you were, but he never even heard my name. But Sergeant Rush took all our names. He knew about Shad, and that Fiona was going home; and you told Jamison Shad was, too. He could have guessed what we'd do next. Between them they had all the information necessary to carry out both attacks.'

Rosie was doing sums. 'This is turning into a major conspiracy, you know. Jamison and Rush, the boatmen, someone to run us off the road, someone to break into your house . . . And that makes no sense unless there was someone waiting at Fee's house as well. That's at least six people in two places three hundred miles apart. That's damn near Mafia proportions!'

Prufrock was bewildered. 'What on earth could Philip Morris have known that was worth not only killing him but killing anyone who might go looking for him?'

Rosie indicated the white car. 'For starters, that the man responsible has bought himself a policeman. That alone is a pretty devastating piece of information.'

'And one we ought to pass on as quickly as possible. But to whom? Do you suppose Rush is the only member of the local constabulary implicated? Would we be wiser turning to another police force? How about the Superintendent in Skipley?'

'Maybe. At least it would stop him passing on information of use to the enemy. He won't want to believe it, but how else could Jamison have got your address?'

Prufrock nodded. 'Then let's get out of here before we draw attention to ourselves. Drive on—the road's circular, it'll bring us back to the gates.'

Which was how they came to be approaching the way out from one direction at the same time that the Range Rover was approaching from the other. There was a certain inevitability about the fact that the vehicles would meet just inside the gate. 'Shit!' said Rosie.

'Well, we can't run without making it perfectly obvious that we're trying to avoid them.' Prufrock thought a moment. 'Stop here. Have you got anything about the size of a camera?'

She had a family-sized block of milk chocolate with only a couple of pieces broken off. Prufrock slipped the sling off his arm and climbed out of the car, looking round in a leisurely way. Framing the bar in his hands he pointed it up at the crag now looming behind them. Then he panned across and mimed taking a snap of Edinburgh. 'Is it working?' he asked without looking round. 'Have they gone yet?'

'I don't think they're convinced.' The white car slowed to a halt as its occupants studied the odd behaviour of the tourist who waited till he was leaving the beauty spot before getting out his camera.

Prufrock let his gaze travel casually round until he could see the two men staring back at him as if they couldn't believe their eyes.

'You're right,' he said, returning unhurriedly to his seat, 'they've spotted us. I suggest a swift departure, because while there aren't many cars that could give this one a thrashing, that is probably one.'

Rosie was nodding distractedly. 'And go where? Rush's nick? What if the rot doesn't stop with him?'

'I can't believe everyone there is involved. We'll be safe as long as enough people notice us arrive.'

'Arthur,' said Rosie, putting the car in gear, 'you can count on me.'

When she hit the gas the Volvo took off like a startled Clydesdale. A second later the Range Rover leapt forward like a stag. On sheer acceleration it had the edge but that second made the difference: the Volvo swept under its prow and swung through the park gates

194

metaphorically if not literally on two wheels.

Jamison had to brake to avoid hitting her, which added another few seconds to her lead. She was in among the city traffic before the Range Rover could catch her. 'Yes!' She thumped the steering-wheel in terse triumph.

But it was premature. Apart from a conference once at the Infirmary, of which she remembered something mildly interesting about cyanosis followed by a monumental pub-crawl, Rosie had come a stranger to this city only twenty hours before. She knew her way round the Royal Mile and Princes Street, and she thought she could go straight to the police station. But missing a turn she found herself in streets she didn't know, and as a non-driver Prufrock could offer only limited help from then on. If she'd gone where he indicated she'd have ended up in the police station right enough, explaining why she was going the wrong way up a one-way street.

By then she had a big white car in her mirror. 'Buggery!' She threw a couple of quick left turns followed by a right, ducked through what was more an entry than a road, saw a parking sign and followed it on the basis that there is no better place to hide a car than among three hundred others.

But after a moment the Range Rover fell into line behind her and what she'd thought of as a haven suddenly became a trap. With an imprecation that made Prufrock blush she spun the wheel, cut across the bows of someone leaving the car-park—much squealing of tyres, blaring of horns, shaking of fists—and took the only route available to a vehicle she'd have spent five minutes eight-point-turning to go back the way she'd come.

Nevertheless it was a mistake. What might have been another alley that joined a proper thoroughfare further on turned out to be the access to a courtyard surrounded by flats. When the Range Rover stopped in the entry it sealed up the courtyard as effectively as a cork does a bottle. 'Fuckety, fuckety, fuckety . . .' whined Rosie, looking desperately for a way out.

If they'd been a couple of teenage boys they'd have got away. Four stairways climbed up the back of the buildings, no doubt others went down the front; if they could have run for it they would quickly have made their escape. But they were a fat middle-aged woman and an old man with his arm in a sling, and they couldn't have beaten a fit young man and a reasonably fit slightly older one over a hundred metres with a fifty metre start. Their only chance was to stay in the car with the doors locked and hope neither man had brought a weapon to a friendly meeting.

Leaving their vehicle blocking the exit the two men crossed the courtyard, separating as they reached the Volvo. Rush came to the driver's window and waited; and when Rosie still didn't lower it, tapped politely.

'Bog off,' she said tersely.

He sighed. 'Ms Holland, there are two ways we can do this. There's the easy way, where you wind down the window and I explain what's going on here, and—'

'And there's the hard way, for which you need a five-ton truck,' said Rosie through her teeth and the glass.

Rush went on as if she hadn't spoken. 'And there's the embarrassing way, where I call my Superintendent and he comes down here and explains what's going on.'

'If you're expecting me to be shocked,' gritted Rosie, 'you're going to be disappointed. I didn't for a moment think this stopped with you.'

'Oh dear,' Rush said mournfully, 'this is most regrettable. You weren't supposed to see us together. No one was. We went up there specially so no one would see us.'

'If you didn't want to be seen,' growled Rosie, 'you shouldn't have met in a car as discreetly understated as the Popemobile.'

By now Malcolm Jamison had appeared at Prufrock's window. He nodded a greeting; Prufrock nodded back.

'What were you doing up there, anyway?'

Rosie barked an ironic little laugh. 'Waiting for you to get back to your office, actually.' It struck her there might be a bit of leverage in that. 'I said I'd be back in half an hour. If I don't show up they'll wonder why.'

Rush shrugged. 'Not really. I'll say I bumped into you while I was out.'

'Look,' said Rosie, waving a hand, her voice rising in spite of herself, 'these flats are full of people. Do you really think they're going to watch while you beat our heads in and nobody's going to pick up the phone to complain about the noise?'

'*What*?' Jamison sounded astonished, and glanced up at the flats as if he'd only just noticed them. Then he looked across the car at Rosie, his handsome face twisting in disbelief.

Rosie saw an opening and went for it. 'Oh, yes. If you're not back in that ice-cream van and out of here in ten seconds flat I'm going to thump this horn, and keep my hand down until either the battery goes flat or you find a way of opening the door. I don't know how strong the Noise Abatement Society is in Edinburgh but my guess is that'll be enough to get them reaching for their phones.'

'Oh yes?' Before she'd finished speaking Jamison had shimmed the lock on the nearside door. He opened it and stood in the aperture, and though he said no more his mere presence was a threat.

There must have been lots of things that a watcher of pulp movies could have done. If she'd reversed the car sharply the open door would have sent Jamison flying; if she'd then . . . But the reality was she was not James Bond, she was a newspaper columnist, and while she was agonizing over her options the moment passed.

DS Rush frowned disapprovingly across the car. 'Will you stop showing off and deal with this?'

Jamison straightened up with a disappointed scowl. 'You're no fun.' He reached inside his jacket.

CHAPTER FOURTEEN

'Immigration?' Rosie thought he was producing a gun from his jacket, would have been less taken aback if he had. This ID card was both anti-climactic and bewildering. 'What on earth is there for Immigration to do here? Surely to God we're not denying admission to Scots now?' That reminded her of something: when she had a little time she'd wonder what.

'If you don't like the policies, tell the government,' Malcolm Jamison said calmly. 'Nobody asks my opinion, except on enforcement. It's like *Ghostbusters*: a door opens somewhere, aliens come through into our world, and it's my job to find it, nail it shut and find out whose pockets are getting lined.'

'Pockets?'

'Pockets is what it's all about,' said Jamison emphatically. 'People who traffic in illegals don't do it out of the goodness of their hearts

199

or because they want to share the British way of
life. They're not sneaking in friends and
relatives, or this really nice Filipina maid who
ironed so beautifully for them on holiday in the
Seychelles. We get all of that, but the real
problem is the multi-million pound operation
bringing in a thousand people a year.

'But it's not like Cook's Tours, there isn't a
courier on every trip to make sure all needs are
catered for. It'll be a journey they'll never
forget, all right, but that's because these are
successful people, they have to be to afford this
option, and they aren't used to being treated
like cattle. Literally: they're packed inside legal
cargoes like calves in veal-crates, and if they get
ill they're ditched along the way. If they're
coming in by boat, that means over the side.

'These are not nice people behind this, Ms
Holland. There's no principle involved—all
they're interested in is profit. You might think
the Home Office is tough on illegal immigrants
but trust me, beside these guys I look like
Albert Schweitzer. They'll kill anyone who gets
in the way—immigrants who give them a
problem, people like me who're trying to stop
them, anyone who stumbles on to anything that
could threaten them. Like you. Like your
friends in Skipley.'

'Like Philip Morris?'

'Ah.'

They had adjourned to the BTW offices,
entering discreetly through the back.

200

Even now she knew, Rosie couldn't see Malcolm Jamison as a government agent; which was, of course, his best defence. There are two ways to tackle organized crime: mob-handed, with officers from all the relevant departments and enough fire-power to protect them, or single-handed. As a nail penetrates further than a hammer, so one man can get closer and learn more about an illicit operation than a full task-force. But it's lonely, dangerous work, and if that was how Jamison made his living Rosie no longer begrudged him his flash car, his soap-ad shirt, his smooth features or his smug manner. The man was entitled.

Now he perched on the windowsill with his legs elegantly crossed and exchanged a significant glance with DS Rush, who shrugged. 'I think you'd better tell her.'

When Jamison still hesitated Rosie gritted: 'I think you'd better tell her, too.'

'All right: some of it. I said Philip was working for me. That wasn't strictly true. There's no such thing as the British Trust for Wildlife—it's me, a rented office and a logo. I didn't know a goshawk from a golden eagle until I moved in here a couple of months ago with my *Observer's Book of Birds*.'

'Two months ago? But—'

'Yes. That's when Philip went missing. That was, in fact, the first thing I did.'

'You kidnapped him?' Rosie's voice soared. 'From his room, at gunpoint, like Shad said?'

Jamison nodded. 'Yes. How did he know?'

Rosie ignored that. 'Why?'

'I needed to get him away quickly, for his own safety. He didn't know me from Adam but he did know he was in danger. I reckoned it was the only way he'd come.'

Very calmly Prufrock said, 'Are you telling us that Philip Morris is alive?'

'Yes, of course,' Jamison answered immediately. 'My God, did you think I'd *killed* him? No wonder you were anxious to avoid us in the park!'

'Then, where is he?'

Jamison smiled coolly. 'Don't be offended, but with the man's life depending on it I'm keeping that information to a select circle: him and me.'

'That's true,' nodded Rush. 'He won't even tell me.'

'So you weren't in this from the start?'

'I came into this,' said the sergeant shortly, 'yesterday afternoon when you people brought me some crazy story about broken windows and forged postcards and a boy who reads tea-leaves. I told you I'd look into it: I came to see what BTW had to say, and Mr Jamison pulled that card of his. Back at the station I got a message that the Assistant Chief Constable had promised the Home Office my full co-operation.

'After last night's events we needed to talk again, but Jamison didn't want to come to the station and he didn't want me coming here. We arranged to meet in the park.' He gave a little saturnine smile. 'Imagine our consternation when . . .'

'Quite.' Prufrock frowned and shook his head. 'But where does Mr Morris fit in? Why was he in danger? Who shot Shad and tried to kill us? Oh, yes,' he added. 'And why should we believe you this time when you've lied like a trooper till now?'

Jamison squinted at him. 'Mr Prufrock, you seem to think I owe you an explanation. I don't. When this is all over I may humour you with one, but until then I'm not prepared to confide in people I hardly know. I've told you Morris is safe; even that could put him at risk if it gets about. You're sure as hell not getting anything else. Now, could you go find some birds of your own to watch? Because I really do have more important things to do than this.'

The way Rosie shot out of her chair—she'd claimed the comfortable one this time—the three men thought she was going to hit Malcolm Jamison. Rush gaped at her; Prufrock stiffened ready to defend her; Jamison himself recoiled on the window-sill, losing both balance and dignity.

But the violence she was stirred to wasn't physical. She leaned across the desk at him, her broad face suffused with anger—not at his rudeness, that she could have dealt with in kind, but at his arrogance. He spoke to them as

203

if they were the biggest problem he faced, as if everything else was under control; as if this whole business was going according to plan and none of it could have been handled any better.

'You've had more important things to do for the last two months,' she spat. 'Like fixing things so Philip can go home to his sister. Like arresting whoever's threatening him. Jesus, Mary and Joseph, like putting an end to this thing, whatever it is, before whoever's behind it wipes out anyone who might know anything! Those are the important things you've had to do, and you haven't done any of them; with the result that last night three people almost died. There's a boy in Skipley General Hospital with a hole in his head because of you.

'You smug bastard! You had every chance to put the brake on this before it left the tracks. You could have taken Fee into your confidence at the start: let Philip call her, put her mind at rest. None of us would have been here if you'd done that. When Fee and I came to see you, when Shad told the police what he'd felt in Philip's room: if you'd come clean then nobody would have got hurt. If you'd shown us that damn card yesterday we'd have gone away and no one would have come after us. If Shad Lucas spends the rest of his life on a ventilator, it'll be your fault.'

If she'd been any less angry Rosie would have known she was being unfair. But the barbs were sharp and struck home: Jamison flushed

204

and went white. He was a man who did a difficult, dangerous job and was given a degree of latitude because of it. He risked his own neck; sometimes it was the only way to get a result. He did it for three reasons: he was well paid, he took pride in doing a job that would have frightened and defeated most men, and he believed he was achieving something worthwhile.

He hadn't gone into the Immigration Department to keep the streets clear and the labour market open for white Anglo-Saxon Protestants—as he understood it, they all originated in the Indus Valley anyway. He did this job, which tended to make him more popular with people he didn't like than with people he did, because illegal immigration was a traffic in human misery. Whatever people in foreign parts thought, the streets of London were paved not with gold but with stone: cold, hard and unyielding. It was tough enough making your way there with everything in your favour, when you could ask for help without fear of being frogmarched on to the next flight out. He genuinely believed that most of the people who risked their lives and spent their money to come here illicitly would have been happier staying at home and shaping their own destinies. He didn't underestimate the task, but not many countries would be worth living in if their most enterprising citizens left as soon as they had a grubstake.

So Malcolm Jamison was not accustomed to feeling like shit because of the job he did. Insults left him unmoved. This was different because of the possibility that the angry woman opposite was right: that his actions were directly responsible for the attack on Shad Lucas's life. The implications swamped him. Brain damage. Hemiplegia; quadriplegia. Loss of self. Never to walk again. Never to lie with a woman again. Never to do anything unaided ever again. If she was right and he'd inflicted that on a young man at the peak of his strength, with all his life to come, the sleek Mr Jamison would have trouble living with himself. He growled, 'That isn't true,' and his voice caught.

Which rather knocked Rosie off her stride. It wasn't the first thing people noticed but she was a compassionate woman. The combination of powerful intellect and forceful personality made her a formidable opponent: she could have mauled this man, left him reeling on the ropes with blood dripping metaphorically from his nose. But she saw now that wouldn't be appropriate. Jamison was no more to blame for what had happened to Shad than she was. If he'd been arrogant, so had she. He'd put his desire to get his job done ahead of his duty to safeguard those involved; so had she. Neither of them needed reminding that two other people might have managed things so nobody got hurt.

She sighed and resumed her seat. 'No,

probably not. I don't know any more. I know this started off as a bit of a puzzle I was helping to solve, and somehow it turned into a war of attrition. But no, I don't think that's your fault. I don't even think it's mine. I'm shouting at you because I don't know the guy who's really to blame.'

Prufrock had deliberately kept quiet while Rosie vented her frustration. But at that he raised frosty periwinkle eyes and pinned Jamison to the window with them. 'Do you?'

'Do I what?'

'Know who's to blame? The man who's smuggling in illegal aliens, who wants Philip dead, who had Rosie and me run off the road, who sent a gunman for Shad. The one you have to arrest before any of us will be safe again. Do you actually know who he is?'

It took Jamison some moments to answer and by then no answer was necessary. 'Yes,' comes out very easily; 'Yes, but I'm not telling you,' takes hardly any longer. 'No,' came out like pulling teeth. He pursed his lips and drew his eyebrows together; then he sniffed; then he gazed up at the ceiling; then he gave a careless shrug that was meant to convey 'Me? Of course! Of course I know.' Then he recrossed his ankles, and folded his arms for good measure, and said, 'No.'

He wouldn't have left it at that. He'd have started the next sentence 'But': 'But I'm close to finding out; But I know someone who does.

But I know how to catch him.' It would have been untrue, at least it would have been premature, but it would have been better for his self-respect than that bald 'No.'

But Prufrock didn't wait for him to elaborate. He nodded. 'That's what I thought. You'd probably better not kick us out, then. Because we do.'

'We do?' Rosie's face was a study in astonishment so her quickly appended, 'That's right, we do!' convinced no one.

'Really?' said Jamison cautiously. 'You want to share that with me?'

'In fact, no.' Prufrock enjoyed having their full attention. 'At least, not until I'm satisfied you'll use the information to good effect.'

'God damn it, that's why I'm here—why I've *been* here for the last nine weeks! You think two months pretending to be a bird-nut is the climax my career has been building up to? Tell me who I need to nail to get back to the real world and I'll light a candle for you in the crypt where the Home Secretary goes to avoid the daylight.'

Prufrock was not so easily won round. 'Words are cheap, Mr Jamison. The fact is you've lied to us not once but again and again. I expect you had your reasons. You may have equally good reasons for letting this man remain at large now—he may lead you to someone even higher up. But that won't do. I want those who hurt my friends behind bars. I can give you the name you need to do that, but my price is that you act against him now. So Philip can go home, and those of us who care about Shad can at least feel that he wasn't just a pawn in your game, sacrificed to keep more important pieces in play.'

Until then Jamison had thought of Prufrock mainly as the old man Rosie Holland had in tow, possibly as a witness, possibly because his day centre was shut this week. He had to reconsider that now. 'Mr Prufrock, if you're in possession of material facts and you choose to withhold them—'

Prufrock chuckled dryly. 'No, Mr Jamison, that won't do either. I'm not trying to impede justice but to hasten it. I know now who sent the van that ran us off the road. I presume that's who you're looking for, and that he's also responsible for your illegal immigrants, the break-in at my house and the attack on Shad. I can give you his name right now. But if all that's going to happen is you watch *him* for two months, I'd rather tell some other law enforcement agency. And/or the newspapers.

'I mean to see this man pay for what he's done to us. If you can also prosecute him under immigration law so much the better, but I won't wait and risk losing him. We end it today, or Rosie's newspaper gets the biggest swoop of its long history.'

'Scoop,' Rosie corrected him, *sotto voce*, but nobody paid any heed.

209

Jamison said quietly, 'I don't like being black-mailed.'

'*I* don't like being lied to.'

It took DS Rush to break the impasse. 'If you don't, someone else'll get the collar and you'll have wasted two months' work,' he murmured.

Jamison had actually worked that out. He was a poker player, his instinct was to bluff his way to success. But not to go for bust when he hadn't the cards to back him. He held Prufrock's gaze a long time; but when the old man yielded nothing, finally the younger one dipped his head. 'All right. But if this goes pear-shaped I'll have you, Mr Prufrock.'

CHAPTER FIFTEEN

One of the unwritten rules of shooting is that, if a gun needs attention, it must never be given it at leisure at the end of the season but in haste before the start of the next. Mid to late summer is thus a busy time for a gun shop.

Geoffrey Monk had barely got rid of one customer before another arrived, and as he left a small man with a bristly moustache, a harassed manner and no gun case came in. 'Mr Monk, I'm sorry to impose on you again. The fact is, I'm in trouble and I don't know who else in this city I can turn to.'

'My dear chap!' Monk quickly lifted the flap

in the counter. 'Come in the back and tell me what the problem is.'

Behind the shop was a tweedy room with antlers on the wall and a sofa smelling of labrador. Prufrock sank on to it gratefully. 'I've made a terrible mistake, and I don't know where to go for help. I certainly can't go to the police.'

Monk's eyes widened in surprise. 'Whatever have you been up to?'

'Nothing criminal, I assure you. But I've got hold of the wrong end of a stick, and people are going to get hurt because of it.'

Monk sat on the other sofa. 'Is this still about the *White Heather*?'

'In a way,' said Prufrock. 'Miss Holland and I were on our way to see the captain when somebody tried to kill us. Ran us off the road, Mr Monk! We're all right, both of us; but whoever was sent to deal with the other half of our party did a better job. I told you my gardener found some evidence in Mr Morris's room? He's been shot. He's not expected to recover.'

Appalled, Monk stared at him. 'In God's name, what's it all about?'

'Illegal immigrants, Mr Monk,' said Prufrock. 'They smuggle foreigners into the country. That boat's involved, and so is the body we understood Mr Morris was working for, the British Trust for Wildlife.'

'BTW?' said Monk faintly. 'Really?'

211

'That's where I got it so badly wrong. I thought they were on the side of the angels. Jamison told us he worked for the Immigration Department. He had an ID card; it looked perfectly genuine, and what he said made sense. He said he was holding Philip as a witness until he was ready to make arrests. I believed him.'

'And now you don't?'

'I know you had your doubts about him. I should have paid more heed. Well, it's clear enough now. There's a young man dying in Skipley General who'd be weeding my rockery if Jamison was who he said he was. If only I'd worked it out sooner! He's not investigating illegal immigration, Mr Monk, he's organizing it! He was the only one, apart from us, who knew Shad and Miss Morris were going home. He knew where Rosie and I were going and where the young people were going, and within a few hours we'd been ambushed and so had they.'

'My God!' whispered Monk.

'But even that's not the worst of it. The detective handling the case is in his pay. We've seen them together. When I thought Jamison was a government agent it seemed reasonable enough. But if Jamison's crooked, so is Detective Sergeant Rush and God alone knows who else. If I go to the police station the best I can expect is being fobbed off until it's too late for me to save them.'

Monk was wallowing in his wake. 'Save who?'

'Mr Morris and Miss Holland.' Prufrock mopped his brow with a handkerchief. 'I'm telling this very badly. You see, I know now what happened to Philip. He stumbled on a smuggling ring and went into hiding: while no one knew where, he was safe. But then ... I told you, we thought Jamison was on our side. We believed that what he was telling us was the truth; in return we told him everything we'd found out. Mr Monk, he and Rosie are on their way to meet Philip right now. When they get there he'll kill them both.'

The stillness in the little tweedy room was such that when Monk exhaled it sounded like wind through trees. 'I see,' he said finally. 'Yes, I do see.' He offered nothing more.

Prufrock pressed on. 'I hoped—I don't know—I can't drive. I need someone to take me there. There's not much time but maybe just enough if you know someone with a fast car who'd save his very natural questions until we're on our way.' He bit his moustache. 'And I hoped you'd lend me a gun.'

Monk stared. 'You're prepared to go that far?'

'I don't have any choice, Mr Monk. This is my fault—my miscalculation. I trusted the man. I thought I'd been so clever, working it all out, I couldn't wait to tell him. And he was so plausible! With the detective backing him up, it never occurred to me to doubt until after Rosie had left with him. But the evidence was there, if only I'd recognized it sooner.

'I couldn't think what to do then. I thought there was no one I could turn to, and then I remembered you.' He shook his head, impatient with himself. 'I can do nothing for Shad, but perhaps I can still save Rosie and Mr Morris. If I can get hold of a gun and a fast car. I have to try.'

'Mr Prufrock, can you even handle a gun?'

'Well, no,' admitted Prufrock. 'But maybe it'll be enough just to have it and look determined.'

'If determination alone would do,' said Monk stoutly, 'I'd lend you one. But professional criminals won't be routed by a pretence, however gallant. So no, I'm not going to give you the means to confront a dangerous man alone.'

'But—'

'What I will do,' continued Monk, a faint sombre smile touching his lips, 'is come with you. I can handle a gun, and as it happens I have a fast car. Give me a minute to get my gear together and we'll be on our way.'

'But . . . Mr Monk.' Prufrock looked astounded. 'I can't ask that of you. He's dangerous and he may have help. I have no choice, I'm responsible for this mess. But I won't risk anyone else's life.'

'Mr Prufrock, I can handle it. We may not

214

have known one another long but if birders can't help one another, God help us all!'

'But ... but ...' stammered Prufrock. 'If only there were more of us! Or if I was thirty years younger.'

'I know a couple of lads I can call, to give us a bit of back-up if we need it.' He returned to the shop for a minute and Prufrock heard muttering on the phone. Then Monk was back. 'Let's go.'

The car was so streamlined Prufrock had trouble getting in. 'Which way?' said Monk as the engine awoke with a growl.

The way was south and the distance was not far; but as they left the main road to follow lanes that climbed into the Moorfoot Hills they quickly found themselves in a wild Midlothian landscape—sheep grazing, a few villages and farms, an ancient church, a copse of trees, ruins on a rocky knoll. 'That's it?' said Prufrock breathlessly.

'That's Crichton Castle,' confirmed Monk. 'This is where Morris is hiding?'

Prufrock nodded. 'He's been here all along, camping in the stable block. If anybody asks he's carrying out work for the Department of the Environment. Actually, he's spent two months watching birds.'

Monk shuddered delicately. 'I think, after two months, I'd be throwing stones at them.'

Prufrock looked shocked. 'We seem to be here first. At least, I don't see a car.' As he spoke one came up the lane behind them. 'Oh no . . .'

Monk shook his head crisply. 'That's my friends.' He got out and walked back to meet them. Monk's 'lads' were a pair of fifteen-stone bruisers.

He saw Prufrock's expression as he returned and chuckled tersely. 'We need protection, I wasn't going to call the Girl Guides. You should be glad to have a couple of strapping young lads backing us up.'

'Oh, I am, Mr Monk,' Prufrock said fervently. 'I am.'

They put both cars out of sight and the strapping young lads stayed with them. Carrying his gun case in one hand and a pistol in the other Monk hurried up the path towards the ruins. Prufrock kept up as best he could.

There were two buildings. The one that wasn't the castle looked more like a chapel than a stable, the high-pitched roof braced by great buttresses. Only a horseshoe window over the door hinted at its real purpose.

Monk headed for the castle. 'We'll wait. I want to have them all together before we show ourselves. Then I can keep them there while you explain the situation.'

'And if Jamison isn't alone?'

'However much help he has they won't be able to cope with guns in front and behind them.'

'Your—lads are armed—too?'

216

'We're all shooting men, Mr Prufrock. Jamison won't know we've never pointed our guns at people before.'

From the outside Crichton was sturdy and squat, a Scottish stronghold against Scottish enmities and Scottish weather; but behind the stout walls was an Italian Renaissance courtyard. A flight of broad stone steps led towards the upper apartments.

'Good heavens!' exclaimed Prufrock.

'The Fifth Earl,' commented Monk absently. He was making his guns ready. 'Fought a lot of duels in Italy.'

'That explains it,' said Prufrock. 'Can I help?'

He got in the way until Monk showed him how to load. 'I hope I won't have to fire. But if things get out of hand it'll speed things up to have a loader.'

'I feel like the colonel's daughter in the cowboy films,' murmured Prufrock.

They found a position overlooking the path. A few minutes passed, then they heard an engine. 'Here we go,' said Monk. 'Keep your head down till I have them covered.'

'You don't need to keep Rosie and Philip covered.'

'I do, until you've had a chance to explain who their real friends are.'

Two figures came down the path. Monk waited but no one else appeared. This was better than he'd dared hope. The woman was

217

Rosie Holland, unmistakable even at this distance, so the man must be Jamison. They headed for the stables.

'Now, Mr Monk?' Prufrock said anxiously.

'Now, Mr Prufrock,' affirmed Monk. With the rifle in his grasp, suddenly he looked less like an Edinburgh shopkeeper and more like a man who made his living with the instruments of death.

* * *

Since they were in no great hurry, Rosie had taken the opportunity offered by the drive out here to apologize to Malcolm Jamison. It was something she had a certain gift for. People who knew her to be brash and opinionated expected her to cling to those opinions obstinately, were surprised to find her generous in defeat. But Rosie had learned that admitting to error cost nothing and could win hearts. It was the price she paid for having a view on every subject under the sun, that when she was wrong she would confess it with good grace. That way people went on listening to what she had to say.

It wasn't exactly an error she had to confess to Jamison, more an error of judgement. 'I've been pretty unpleasant to you, haven't I? Sorry about that. I thought you were a crook. When you were so evasive about where Philip was and how we could contact him, I was just about convinced you'd disposed of him. I knew you were lying, I assumed you must be guilty of something. The idea that Philip might have been kidnapped at gunpoint in his own best interests simply never occurred to me.'

Jamison was in danger of falling under Rosie's spell as Matt Gosling, Gerry Fish from the Palmyra Café, and others had before him. Her honesty was seductive. He shrugged. 'I can see it wouldn't be the first thing that came to mind. My problem was, the more I tried to convince you there was nothing to worry about, the more lies I ended up telling. No wonder you found it less than persuasive.'

'I still don't understand,' she said, watching him out of the corner of her eye. Another thing an apology was good for was oiling other people's tongues. 'You came here to snatch Philip to safety, yes? So it wasn't your activities he stumbled on to. So how did he get involved? What made him a marked man?'

Jamison sighed. Rebuffing Rosie Holland was like trying to keep out bees with chicken-wire. In the end it was easier to satisfy her curiosity than to keep fending her off. Besides, now it hardly mattered. He was committed, they all were, to a course of action that would bring matters to a speedy conclusion. If that was a bad decision, the least of his worries was that she might spread the story he was about to tell.

'It was a sheer fluke that Morris got

involved. You know he was watching birds in The Minch that fortnight before he disappeared? So he's sitting on a rock with his high-powered binoculars and his zoomlens camera, and early one morning a boat comes up through the Sound of Mull. She's the *White Heather* out of Oban. He's hitched rides on her at different times, he'd have used her this trip if someone with a yacht hadn't given him a lift. She's heading for Barra at the southern tip of the Hebrides.

'The birds weren't doing much that morning,' he continued, 'so Philip watched the *White Heather* for a change. There was a container ship hove to off Barra Head. Haldane came alongside and through his glasses Philip saw people being lowered on to the *White Heather*. Then the ship headed out to sea while Haldane returned inshore and disappeared up one of the Knoydart sea-lochs. An hour later he was on his way back towards Oban.

'Now, Morris may be a crank but he's no fool,' said Jamison. 'Cruises to the Highlands and Islands don't use old container ships and don't send their clients on shore excursions by lowering them on a rope. No, he'd seen something no one was meant to see, and it didn't take him long to work out what.'

'Illegal immigrants being landed,' whistled Rosie, though by then it hardly counted as a feat of deduction.

220

Jamison nodded. 'I don't know what he'd have done if that had been the end of it. Maybe nothing: not everyone thinks it's a big deal. He might have thought good luck to them and kept quiet. But when his time on the rock was up his yachtie friend was enjoying himself in Stornoway and the Oban piermaster sent the *White Heather* to collect him instead.'

When Captain Haldane realized where Philip Morris had been camping, though neither of them spoke of it he knew his rendezvous with the ship had probably been observed. He could do nothing immediately— if he'd returned without Philip the piermaster would have wanted to know why. So they landed at Oban and Philip left for home.

'Near Crianlarich he had an encounter pretty much like yours,' said Jamison. 'A white panel van forced him off the road. He wasn't hurt, but two large gentlemen with tyre-irons flung him in the back of the van. Which was packed with Chinese men, women and children wearing Marks & Spencer T-shirts and practising their Scottish accents.'

'Chinese!' exclaimed Rosie, and Jamison looked at her oddly.

'Chinese,' he confirmed. 'Well, they shuffled up so he could sit down—'

'They are very polite,' murmured Rosie; then seeing his expression, 'Sorry—something I just remembered. Carry on.'

Philip asked where they'd come from and

221

they said Hong Kong. They'd done well under British capitalism, didn't want to be there when the communists took over. They'd expected the twenty-eighth and last governor would win them the right to settle in Britain. He tried. In September 1995 Chris Patten said there was a moral and economic case for giving rights of abode to three and a half million Hong Kong residents; but the British Government didn't agree. People who'd spent years thumbing their noses at Beijing finally realized it was going to happen; they were going to be left behind when the British went home. Unless they made other arrangements.

'In Hong Kong just about anything is possible if you have money,' said Jamison. 'There are more Rolls Royces per head of population there than here; every month fifteen thousand people buy a mobile phone. The colony is one giant Ways & Means Committee: if you have the means, someone'll find a way. With people willing to pay big money to beat the '97 handover it was inevitable that pipelines would be set up. We were watching for them. We missed this one because it didn't come in anywhere we'd thought of.'

Taking Philip for one of their couriers the migrants had described the stages of their journey: a boat out of Hong Kong, a couple of flights, the container ship that had brought them from Liberia and the *White Heather* that had ferried them ashore.

'Nobody's going to challenge the comings and goings of a local fishing boat,' said Jamison. 'The van meets it at some isolated beach and distributes the illegals round the towns and cities where they're left to sink or swim. A lot of them swim. They have contacts here who help them settle in, find jobs where not too many questions will be asked, get their kids into school. Give them a couple of years and they'll be as successful here as they were in Hong Kong. But some of them get into trouble, need help, find themselves talking to policemen. That's when my phone rings.'

But Rosie wasn't as interested in the general as the specific. 'So Philip's in the back of a van surrounded by Hong Kong Chinese calling themselves Ian. What happened next? Why didn't the large gentlemen with the tyre-irons just hit him behind the ear and roll him into a ditch?'

'Fortunately, they didn't reckon to have the authority, decided to hold him and await instructions. But when the van stopped to let off some passengers in Ayr he made a run for it. The last thing two guys with a van full of illegals need is a scene, so they drove off.'

At first Philip Morris hadn't even known where he was. It had been late evening and no one would help him: they had thought he was drunk, maybe dangerous. He was wearing shorts, plimsoles and a bobble hat. Eventually someone had called the police.

At the station the desk sergeant had also thought he was drunk until Morris had insisted on being breathalyzed. Then he had called an inspector and Philip had told *him* what had happened.

'He contacted the Home Office, they called my boss and he called me,' said Jamison. 'But it's four hundred miles from London and when I got to Ayr Morris had gone. He'd made his statement and set off for home. To be fair, it was nine hours since he'd jumped out of the van. He must have thought he was being held till there was a padded cell free. But it was a bad move. A police station was the safest place for a man who'd seen too much to be left alone.'

Jamison followed him to Edinburgh. 'I wasn't sure he'd have got that far, or maybe I'd find him dead in his bath. Instead I found him packing to visit his sister.'

'So you pulled a gun on him?' Rosie's voice soared. She coughed it down. 'Are you sure you work for Immigration?'

Jamison looked rueful. 'That's what my chief said. Slightly more hysterical, maybe. I didn't have much choice. He'd already walked out of protective custody: he thought all he had to do was lie low for a bit, didn't understand that if he went to his sister both of them would be in danger. But I knew what these people would do to protect themselves, and I knew they couldn't

224

be far behind. I had to get him out, quickly, quietly and over the back wall. Pointing my gun at him was the best way to avoid an argument.' He shrugged. 'I'm issued with the thing to save lives. That's what I used it for.'

Rosie blinked; but as someone who regularly let ends justify means she wasn't best qualified to criticize. 'So you got him to safety, and you explained all this to him, and he agreed to lie low until you could arrest those involved. So what were you waiting for? He's been missing two months—more, now. You couldn't keep him forever. And why didn't you at least tell his sister?'

'I did,' scowled Jamison. 'Or I thought I had. Morris said she'd be expecting a postcard so I told him to write one and I'd post it where it couldn't give away his location. So what did the stupid sod do but describe all the birds he could see? *I* could have found him from that. So I rewrote the message, without the iffy bits, on a card from Shetland and had it posted there. I'm not a professional forger but it looked pretty good to me. I thought the signature would clinch it. I never imagined I'd have to get it past a psychic.'

'When Prufrock called BTW you denied knowing Philip. Then you said he was working for you under another name. What was all that about?'

'The same—trying to keep the guy safe. Someone I've never heard of comes on making

225

enquiries about him, of course I deny having him! When it turned out you people were acting for his sister I had to give you something: that was all I could come up with at short notice. You should have bought it. What kind of a suspicious sod sees conspiracies behind every cock-up?'

'The sort who's had wool pulled over her eyes often enough to know the smell of sheep,' said Rosie wryly.

CHAPTER SIXTEEN

They left the car at the end of the lane and walked towards the castle. Rosie was still talking, asking questions; by now it was more nerves than curiosity. 'How long would it have gone on if Prufrock hadn't forced your hand? When would Philip have got home?'

Jamison kept his voice low. 'When I'd rounded up the people who need him dead. I didn't know who was behind it. I knew the rest—the *White Heather*, the container ship, the van—and we've picked up a lot of the illegals. But till Prufrock dropped his bombshell I still didn't know who was running this end of the operation. I was scared that if I jumped and missed him he'd vanish and start up again somewhere else.'

'Meanwhile the weeks went by.'

'I was getting close,' Jamison said

defensively. 'A ship comes in twice a month: I know that because every fifteen days or so there's one when Haldane won't take me birding. That was why I set up BTW: for an excuse to hire the *White Heather* on a regular basis. If I'd asked about his activities Haldane would have known I was on to him. But if I ask him to take me out to some rock or other and make a note of the days he puts me off I get the same information without arousing suspicion. The next ship's due in four days. I've got some sophisticated electronics: once I plant them on the van I can track its movements and eavesdrop on conversations in the cab. I hoped, one way or the other, that would lead me to the man in charge.' He sniffed, disappointed. 'It doesn't look as if I shall need them now.'

Rosie shook her head. 'I'm amazed Captain Haldane was willing to hire his boat out. Why would he take the risk?'

'He needed a cover as much as I did. The illegals are how he makes his money but that's only two days a month: if *White Heather* lay around the rest of the time people would ask why. It suited him to have a deal with some bird-nut from out of town that gave him regular employment without interfering with his obligations. He never suspected I was spying on him. He kept his distance; we never got friendly. He didn't much like having me aboard, but I don't think he ever suspected me.' He barked a little laugh. 'I wouldn't be here now if he had.'

Still Rosie was puzzled. 'If you knew about the boat from Philip, why did you set up shop in Edinburgh? You'd have been better off in Oban.'

He raised a sardonic eyebrow. 'Where Haldane could watch every move I made? I wouldn't have fooled him for long if he'd seen how little bird-watching I did when I wasn't with him. Plus, he mightn't have worked for someone he saw too much of. He felt safer waving me off back to Edinburgh than if I'd been staying locally. In fact I spent more time on the West Coast than he ever knew. But as long as my office and answering machine were in Edinburgh he assumed I was, too.'

Rosie nodded appreciatively. 'Clever. And sneaky, which you probably consider a higher compliment.' Jamison grinned, until she added, 'What a pity, after all that work, to be out-thought by a genuine bird-watcher whose knowledge of the criminal mind-set was acquired teaching at a minor public school.'

They'd reached the stable block and stood looking up at the horseshoe window. Jamison said softly, 'Are you ready?'

Rosie nodded again, tersely. 'Uhhuh,' she lied.

But the investigator hesitated, and when she looked at him he was chewing his lip. 'He's not going to blow this, is he—Prufrock? Only, considering it as an intellectual exercise is one

228

thing: carrying it out, with real guns uncomfortably close to your spinal cord, is another. If he loses his nerve and panics he could get any or all of us killed. If that's likely to happen it would be helpful to know now.'

Rosie considered a moment. 'I haven't known him much longer than you have, but I don't think Arthur Prufrock's the panicking kind.'

Anyway, it was too late now to vary the plan as agreed. She raised her voice. 'Philip? Philip Morris? My name's Rosie Holland, I'm a friend of Fee's. I'm here to take you home. Can we come inside?'

'A bit louder,' murmured Jamison. 'There's a jackdaw back at the church might not have heard you.'

'I'm nervous,' Rosie whispered reproachfully.

'*You're* nervous? Who do you think's going to catch the first bullet?'

'Oh, Jesus,' she moaned.

Jamison's hand between her shoulderblades pushed her firmly into the stables. He did this job because at some point it had appealed to him, even if he couldn't always remember why. She, on the other hand, had been caught up in events she hadn't understood well enough to consent to. She wasn't pretending to be scared, that was the genuine article. 'Don't worry, I'll look after you.'

'Unless you catch the first bullet.'

229

'In that case you can look after me and DS Rush can look after you.'

'I don't want to alarm you,' said Rosie grimacing, 'but DS Rush doesn't appear to be here.'

'He's at the church right now, reading their rights to Monk's heavies. Then he'll come up here, and then it'll all be over. Five minutes from now we'll be on our way home.'

'Unless Prufrock's wrong, Monk really is here only to help, and someone else is running the immigration racket.'

'Prufrock', said Jamison firmly, 'had better *not* be wrong.'

Tip-toeing across the cropped turf Geoffrey Monk could see a man's back in the doorway and hear the mutter of conversation. He glanced round but there was only Prufrock: his associates were keeping out of sight and Jamison seemed not to have brought any. There was no reason to wait longer. He raised the rifle and his voice. 'Will you all come outside, please? We need to talk to you.'

There was a hiatus of a few seconds, though it seemed longer. Then Jamison turned slowly on his heel, saw the rifle and instinctively froze. Rosie appeared in the doorway beside him.

'And Mr Morris.' The rifle was at Monk's shoulder as he stepped forward, Prufrock at his heel. 'Tell him it's all right, Mr Prufrock. Tell him there's been a misunderstanding but it's all right for him to come out now. Tell him to

230

come out, Mr Prufrock.'

Quite softly, so that his voice would never have reached inside the building, Prufrock said, 'Philip Morris isn't here.'

For a moment Monk seemed not to have heard him. He went on gazing down the rifle barrel at Jamison, ensuring his hands went nowhere he might have concealed a gun. Then he said, his voice oddly flat, 'What do you mean?'

'He isn't here. He never was here. He *is* watching birds, but not these birds. As Mr Jamison pointed out, Philip is his best witness. He'd be crazy to risk him in'—he gave a coy little cough'—'a half-arsed pantomime like this.' He glanced around. 'The reason we came to Crichton, Mr Monk, is that this place can be secured and innocent bystanders kept at a safe distance in a way that would have been difficult in Edinburgh. The police have us surrounded. Your friends are already under arrest.'

Someone had moved the goal-posts while Geoffrey Monk wasn't looking. It would be some moments before he could take in the full import of what the old man was saying, but he knew better than to drop his guard while he was thinking about it. He backed off a few steps to put all three of them in his sights. His eyes scanned between them like radar. He knew everything had changed, even if he still wasn't quite sure how.

Prufrock obeyed the peremptory gesture of

the rifle and moved beside Jamison. 'There's nothing you can do, you know,' he said softly. He'd once talked a distraught third-former down from the belltower window: with certain differences, the main one being the gun pointed at his chest, this was a similar sort of task. 'Mr Jamison really is with Immigration. He knows what you're involved in, and now it's over. All that remains is to phone your solicitor. Give me the guns and go with Detective Sergeant Rush. That's him coming down the path now.' He looked past Monk's shoulder. 'The man in front; I'm not acquainted with the others.'

Monk also knew better than to spin round and look. 'Inside. Now!' They backed obediently into the stables and he followed; when he glanced behind there were indeed half a dozen men he didn't recognize hurrying towards them. He shouted, 'Stay back, I'm armed!' and had the satisfaction of seeing them scatter.

'Now,' he said tightly, returning his attention to the people in front of him. They'd spread out: he waved the gun to bunch them against the wall. A swift survey of the dim interior showed him no tent, no pile of belongings that a man would need for an extended stay, no other man. 'Prufrock, tell me what's going on.'

Prufrock obliged. 'It had to be you. It could have been both Mr Jamison and Sergeant Rush, but not once we knew Jamison works for the investigation branch of the Immigration Department. One rotten apple you could believe in, but a pair of rotten apples bribing each other?

'The only other person who had all the information necessary was you. I should have realized,' he said in self-reproach, 'when your assassin went to my house. I didn't give my address to anyone, but I left you my phone number when I first called you. With that you could find out where I lived; and there you could get the name and address of my gardener. That's what your associate was looking for when he was disturbed.'

Monk didn't confirm or deny it. But if it hadn't been true, thought Rosie, he'd have been spluttering in horrified indignation by now. Instead of which he just kept gazing steadily down the blue-steel barrel. 'Go on.'

So Prufrock did. 'It was me, wasn't it, who told you Shad found something in Philip's room. That was stupid. I had no reason to suspect you at that point but I should still have been more careful than that. If I'd painted a bull's eye on his T-shirt I couldn't have made him more of a target.'

For a moment the grief threatened to overwhelm him and he stopped, the moustache quivering. All Rosie's instincts were to go to his side and take his hand. But as she moved the rifle swung in her direction and Jamison pressed her behind him.

233

Anyway, Prufrock shook his head. 'It's all right. I'm all right now.' He took a deep breath. 'Did he mean to kill Shad, the man you sent, or only to drag out of him what he knew? Your first priority was to discover where Philip was hiding: you must have hoped that was what Shad had found out. The other thing you needed to know was whether or not Philip had told anyone why he had to disappear. It was vital to establish how badly you were compromised, how many people you had to silence before you'd be safe.

'Ideally, I suppose, your man would have gone to Shad's flat for a lengthy, uninterrupted chat with him. There'd have been the time and the privacy there to do the job properly, get whatever information he had, beat it out of him if he had to, and to finish it how you wanted it finished. But when Matt Gosling and then Shad himself turned up he had to play it by ear. The best he could manage, in the lane with the police already on the way, was to shoot and run.

'I told you Shad was dying. That isn't true. We have every confidence that he'll recover. He'll identify your associate, and he in turn will identify you because by then he'll be looking for concessions.' He paused significantly. 'Unless you identify him first, in which case the concessions will be yours.'

Geoffrey Monk hadn't made a success of two different jobs, running a gun shop and smuggling illegal immigrants, by being a stupid man. He'd spent the last minutes thinking instead of getting angry. Clearly the pipeline was finished. Those who worked for him were now or would soon be helping with police enquiries. He could not return to Cramond.

But he might still escape. He had money abroad; there would be no difficulty making a life for himself elsewhere; his family could join him if they chose to. If he could find a way off this hillside. To that end he had five things going for him: two guns and three hostages.

All the vague amiability was gone as if it had never been. His eyes on Jamison's face were steely. 'You: you're the pro. You have a gun, yes?'

Jamison shook his head. 'No.'

Monk repeated it icily. 'You have a gun, yes?'

Jamison exhaled slowly. 'Yes.'

'Take it out, carefully, with your left hand. Fingertips only. Take out the clip; throw the clip away to the right and the gun to the left. That's better. Now, as a pro, you know I'll kill you all if I have to and not if I don't. So you convince the police. Tell them we're leaving here in five minutes, and if anyone tries to stop us I'll shoot the woman.'

Rosie felt herself grow ashen and her knees turn to string. Jamison was nowhere near as broad as she but he did his best to shield her. His voice was low and utterly serious. 'You must know that isn't going to happen. I can agree, no problem, I can say I'll do anything you want. But the police won't go along with it because they can't. Even if it costs lives. They can't let a man as dangerous as you go free.'

Monk shook his head crisply. 'Don't read the text-book at me. I know what it says. I also know that, down here on the ground, things get done differently sometimes because no one wants to be responsible for a bloodbath. That's why you set up this whole charade: to take me without bloodshed. Only now you can't. I'm not asking for a free pardon. I'm not suggesting that you give up on me, only that you accept it's not going to be today. Another time, another place, maybe. You know who I am. I'll try to disappear but maybe you'll find me anyway. Tomorrow, or the next day, or a month from now. But not today; not here.

'Tell the police to back off. Tell them their chance will come but if they don't get off-side right now I'm going to start shooting, and I'm going to start with her.' Then he thought better of that and his gaze slid sideways. 'No, the old man. If I only get a crack at one of you, that's what'll give me the most satisfaction.'

Malcolm Jamison was a brave man, at times recklessly so, but he would never have agreed to any plan which involved him and two civilians staring up the barrel of a gun. He'd thought it would be over by now. He expected that when Monk realized he'd been tricked he

236

would yield to the overwhelming odds. He knew, of course, that no one who'd distinguished himself in the world of organized crime could be trusted. But Monk was a plotter rather than a man of action: he'd set up and run a clever, profitable operation essentially by means of long-distance phone calls and international banking. He did the hiring, left others to do the firing. The man was a shopkeeper, a bird-watcher for heaven's sake! Faced with certain capture Jamison had expected him to surrender and hire the best lawyer in Scotland. Except in the courts, he had not expected him to make a fight of it.

Perhaps he should have remembered precisely what it was the shopkeeper sold. It altered his whole perspective. Now the mouse had roared, and what Jamison did next depended on Prufrock. He looked at the old man urgently, seeking a clue, but Prufrock was gazing at Monk, his blue eyes wide.

'Goodness me,' he said, taken aback, 'there's no need to get personal. Being on opposite sides doesn't mean we can't behave like gentlemen. If we'd met some other way we might even have been friends. We could have gone shooting. I could have loaded for you.'

The words sank slowly through the still air inside the stone building. Peering past Jamison's shoulder Rosie saw unease flicker across Monk's face as he tried to fathom their meaning. Was there one? Was it just verbal diarrhoea from the anxiety? But Prufrock was a precise, even prissy old man, a man who would choose his words carefully even under stress. Monk needed to know precisely what he'd meant by that, and he needed to know now. The gun was rocksteady on Prufrock's heart. 'Explain.'

There was a note of apology in Prufrock's little sigh. 'I handled your guns after you did. That rifle is empty.'

'You're bluffing.'

'No.'

'No?' Monk regarded him uncertainly, his head tilted to one side, a tiny frown drawing his brows together. Then he gave a little shake of his head, and then he pulled the trigger.

There wasn't time for Rosie to think, What if he's got it wrong? What if there is a shot in the breach? The space between pulling the trigger and the round detonating is imperceptible so she must have thought these things before, when she guessed what Monk was going to do. Still there seemed to be a moment between the fall of the hammer and what came next in which the universe held its breath. Then . . .

Well, nothing. Monk was left holding a beautifully crafted weapon, accurate in the right hands to millimetres over half a mile, that in the absence of something to fire was only an expensive stick. He drew a deep breath and lowered it. 'You weren't bluffing.'

'No,' agreed Prufrock. 'Though feel free to

shoot me with the pistol as well, just to be sure.'

Monk twitched a cold smile. 'I don't believe I will.'

'No, perhaps better not. If by any chance I did leave a round in the chamber, the superglue I squeezed up the barrel would blow it apart in your hand.'

CHAPTER SEVENTEEN

When all the questions were answered and the statements made, and Detective Sergeant Rush had arranged a Press conference at which a version of events was given so guarded it wouldn't have prejudiced the trial of Jack the Ripper, it was noon on Saturday and they still weren't free to leave. Philip Morris had yet to be restored to his anxious sister.

'I can have him here by evening,' said Malcolm Jamison, who'd kept out of the way while the Press were in the police station. 'If Miss Morris flies up this afternoon she could meet him here, which would be rather nice.' He didn't say so but he was thinking the reunion might be worth a photograph. A man could work in the shadows and still enjoy a little public recognition. 'Or we can put him on a Birmingham flight and she can meet him at that end an hour later.'

'I'll phone her and ask. Er . . .' Rosie was doing mental sums. 'Where is he, that it's going

239

to take five hours to get him here?'

Jamison smirked. 'St Kilda. It's where the British Isles fall off the map into the North Atlantic. There's not much there, only a military base, some sheep that eat seaweed and—'

'Don't tell me,' groaned Rosie. 'Some really interesting birds?'

'Puffins. Britain's largest colony apparently.' He shrugged. 'Short of locking him in the Tower of London he was going to be as safe there as anywhere. Nobody would look for him there, and half the time the weather's too rough to land anyway. I'm sending an RAF Sea King for him but even they mightn't make it first try. They'll attempt air-sea rescues in most conditions but I'm not having them risk their necks running a taxi service.'

Fee was still at Alex's flat. She knew by now that her brother was safe and Shad had been shot: relief and a terrible guilt warred in her until she hardly knew where she was. Alex took her to the hospital but she saw nothing to reassure her. More than anything else she needed to keep occupied. 'I'll come up there.'

They met her off the plane. Jamison took them to a private room to wait. They spent the time catching up on one another's news.

'You saw Shad this morning?' said Prufrock. Now he was feeling guilty about what he had said to Monk: not because it was a lie, since lies in a good cause were only little white ones, but

240

because it might be tempting fate. 'How was he?'

Fee gave a despairing little shrug. 'I don't know. The staff kept saying, Don't worry, it's not as bad as it looks; but, oh God! he looked terrible. I can't bear it. He'd have been fine if he'd never met me. He'd have been digging someone's garden today. Thanks to me he's fighting for his life instead.'

'We all contributed,' said Rosie gently. 'But the blame lies with those who meant him harm: the man who ordered him shot and the one who shot him. We're all sorry how things turned out but none of us did anything we could have known would lead to this. There was nothing wrong with your motive, to help someone you loved who was in trouble. There wasn't much wrong with mine. We couldn't have known what we were getting into. Damn it, Shad's the psychic and even he didn't see this coming!'

She hoped that was true. She hoped he hadn't foreseen this and come along anyway, afraid of disappointing them. She remembered again that odd, frightened expression that flitted across his face when Prufrock introduced them. She hoped to God he hadn't known then that she would be the death of him.

'You can't blame the butterfly,' murmured Prufrock. They stared at him, mystified. 'The one that flaps its wings in the Brazilian rain-forest and causes a hurricane in the Caribbean:

you can't blame it for the deaths of fifteen Puerto Rican fishermen and a school-crossing patrol lady in Key West. It was only being a butterfly. It couldn't do other than it did.'

A little later Prufrock found Jamison regarding him with half a smile. 'Sorry, did I miss something?'

'Do you ever?' parried Jamison. 'Chaos theory, hm? You're a surprising man, Mr Prufrock.'

'For a geriatric ex-schoolmaster, you mean.'

Jamison demurred but didn't actually deny it. 'You certainly had Monk fooled. It'll be a while before he looks at a white moustache and thinks "harmless" again. When did you realize he was our man?'

'To be honest, only as we were talking in your office. Not long before that we really did think it was you. But if it wasn't then it had to be someone who'd dealt with me rather than Rosie, which meant a birder.'

'It really was that lucky? It was a sheer fluke that you contacted him?'

'Absolutely. I was calling round the birding fraternity, starting with people I knew and moving on to people they suggested and people those people knew. Someone mentioned Geoffrey Monk and I called him. He'd nothing helpful to say, for reasons which are fairly obvious now, but he said he'd call if he heard anything so I left my number. Then I paid him a visit when we came here. He wasn't the only

242

one, but it was sheer luck that he was one of them.'

'I suppose', ruminated Jamison, 'bird-watching was as good a cover for his activities as it was for mine. Gave him an excuse to skulk round desolate bits of coastline with binoculars. Maybe before all this he knew nothing about birds either.'

'Quite possibly,' agreed Prufrock. He hadn't forgiven the man for even thinking of throwing stones.

'Did you really squirt superglue down his barrels?'

'Oh yes. There's a paper shop next door to his. Belt and braces, you know: I thought he'd let me load for him, but if not all I had to do was distract him for a few seconds and the deed was done.'

'I could be wrong here,' said Jamison, 'but it's my guess you know a little more about guns than you let on.'

'I was a soldier in the Second World War, Mr Jamison. Most men of my age were. We may never have been crack shots but our lives depended on knowing our weapons. Though much is taken,' he observed pontifically, 'much abides.'

'Oh, yes,' said Malcolm Jamison softly. 'I can see how people might underestimate you.'

Prufrock was saved the need to reply by the racket of rotors beyond the window as the lumbering giant of a military helicopter settled

243

on to the concrete apron. As he watched the blades began to slow, a hatch opened and a set of steps appeared. A man appeared at the top of the steps. He was tall and thin, over his shoulder was a rucksack, and he was still wearing an anorak and a bobble hat.

Fee left the terminal at a run and didn't stop until she'd flung herself into an embrace as long-limbed as a spider's. Morris's rucksack fell on the concrete with the solid thump of books and his bobble hat flew off and was whipped away by the rotor-generated wind. Underneath was the long face and kindly expression of an intelligent goat.

Philip was so tall, and Fee so short, that even to kiss the top of her head he had to lift her till her toes were dangling. 'Miss me?'

It wasn't just his words, though they were singularly ill chosen. Fee had been worried sick, first about him, then about Shad, for so long that her emotions were in tatters, shredded and unreliable. She went from relief to fury in the blink of an eye.

'You bastard!' she cried, pummelling his chest. 'You useless frigging bastard! How dare you do this to me?!'

'Me?' He put her down, staring in astonishment. 'Fee, none of this was of my choosing.' He recognized Jamison standing behind her and nodded. 'That's the man you want a word with. He pointed a gun at me: what was I supposed to do, argue?'

'You could at least have let me know you were all right!'

'I did,' said Philip Morris indignantly. 'I wrote you a postcard. Don't tell me you never got it?'

For weeks she'd thought of little else but seeing him again; for a substantial part of that time she'd doubted she ever would. Now he was back, almost like a miracle, and this was the second unfortunate remark he'd made in under a minute.

A little later Rosie would take him aside and explain how that card, with its ornithological indiscretions so unwise that Jamison had felt obliged to forge a new one, had been the catalyst that got all of them involved, especially the injured man who was missing this reunion. Until then Philip Morris hadn't the least idea why his sister should have squirmed out of his grasp, her face hot with rage and tears, and stalked back towards the terminal building, shouting over her shoulder, 'I don't care what you watch from now on, Philip Morris, or where you go to watch it, but don't you dare send me another postcard ever again!'

*   *   *

A nurse showed them to one of the cubicles in ICU. She began, 'Try not to be too alarmed by—'

'I'm a pathologist,' Rosie interrupted

245

shortly.

'In that case,' said the nurse, changing tack smoothly, 'don't get your hopes up. This one's a keeper.'

Rosie saw Prufrock's puzzlement, realized what he was thinking, forestalled his well-intentioned explanation with one of her own. 'No, they know he's a gardener. What she means is, he's not going to die.'

'Ah.' Prufrock gave the nurse an apologetic little smile. 'Sorry.'

'In here.'

It was Sunday morning now, sixty hours since someone had stood close enough to Shad Lucas to touch his face and had shot him instead. But for the sedation he might already have been awake; or he might have been lying just as still and white in the high hospital bed.

The instruments he was coupled to might know which but Rosie couldn't tell by looking at him. All she could see was a strong young body lying motionless under a sheet, an IV-line taped into the back of one hand, electrodes glued to his bare chest. Half his face was hidden by a dressing that covered not only the wound in his cheek but the eye above it; the other eye was closed and bruised-looking. An air-line fed him oxygen.

Prufrock was clearly shocked. 'Oh, dear,' he murmured faintly. 'Dear me!'

'Don't be put off by the hardware,' said Rosie. 'It's all doing useful things for him.

Corpses are much tidier than people who can still benefit from high-tech care.'

They stood watching him for a few minutes. Nothing changed. Prufrock said softly, 'Do you suppose they'll get him?'

Rosie knew who he meant. 'They might. Monk sure as hell wasn't going to protect him, was he? I think if Jamison had offered him extra sugar in his porridge he'd have co-operated. But I expect the name's a false one, and the number Monk called is an answering service, and anyway he's in the country illegally so there'll be no records to trace him by. But he's on the run now, and men on the run make mistakes. I bet they get him eventually.'

'Isn't it extraordinary,' said Prufrock, shaking his head in wonder, 'that you can pick up the phone in Edinburgh and order a murder in the Midlands four hours later? Like ordering a pizza.'

'Or a Chinese take-away,' Rosie said with a wry smile. 'Monk was lucky. Well, he was lucky and he was clever. He realized that among the economic migrants and political refugees who didn't fancy living under the communists there'd be people whose primary object was to escape the attentions of a totalitarian police. It's different from being a criminal in a democracy: authoritarian governments don't require the same standards of proof, don't worry as much about convicting innocent men and use execution to shortcut the appeals procedure.

'Monk watched for people like that coming through the pipeline and made sure he knew where they ended up, and when he came to need a favour he knew where to look. Four hours, though, that's pretty spectacular. It takes me longer than that to get a plumber.'

Prufrock shuddered. 'It's a different world, isn't it? I don't mean Hong Kong. I mean, when people are willing to commit murder to protect an investment. A man like Monk. He had a good business, an enviable standard of living. He didn't need to get involved in anything illegal. Now he's going to prison for maybe fifteen years, and I don't understand why the cherry meant so much to him when he already had the cake.'

'That's because you're a good man, Arthur Prufrock, and basically Gerald Monk is a bad one. Of course you don't understand him.' Rosie grinned. 'It didn't stop you out-thinking him, though, did it?'

He shrugged. 'I couldn't let him get away with this.' He nodded at the bed. 'Oh, Rosie. Will he be all right?'

She wasn't going to lie to him. 'I don't know. But everything that can be done for him is being done, and in the short time I've known him he never struck me as a quitter. My guess is he'll come through OK.'

'But what does that *mean*? That he'll live? Or that in a few weeks he'll be trimming my topiary again?'

She shook her head, defeated. 'Arthur, I don't know.'

Time crawled by, and though crises came and went elsewhere in ICU, sometimes involving considerable bustle and noise, all of it went unnoticed by a young man so deeply unconscious that in the hour she sat with him the only movement Rosie could detect was the fractional rise and fall of his chest.

Finally she decided there were things she could more profitably be doing. As she got up to leave she met Fee Morris coming in.

'Any news?'

Rosie shook her head. 'Still waiting. How's Philip?'

'He's fine. He's catching up on his sleep. I thought I'd come and see . . .' She didn't finish the sentence.

'Sure. Go in and keep him company.'

Fee forced a little unhappy smile. 'We were going to spend some time together, but this wasn't what I had in mind. A date—that was his price for helping me. I don't know, it was kind of serious and kind of not, but that's what he said and I agreed. We thought we might go dancing.' The sapphire eyes grew moist. 'It might be premature to take my little black dress to the dry-cleaners just yet, don't you think?'

Rosie took the girl by the shoulders, captured her gaze. 'Fee, I don't believe that young man is finished. When two doctors say that he satisfies the brain-death criteria I'll believe it, not before. I don't know whether he'll dance again. I don't know whether he'll walk again. But until he's finally and officially dead, I doubt there's a man born who wouldn't appreciate the sight of you in a little black dress. Get it cleaned, get it on and get back here. I can't think of a more powerful incentive to get well for Shad Lucas or any man with a gram of testosterone still circulating.'

Fee chuckled and felt a tear slip down her cheek. 'OK. But I'd like to sit with him for a bit first.'

'He'd like that, too.'

CHAPTER EIGHTEEN

Rosie headed for the office. It was Sunday morning, no one would be there; she could catch up on a bit of paperwork and think what she was going to say at the inevitable inquest.

She offered to drive Prufrock home first but he thought he'd stay at the hospital a while longer. There was a policeman waiting, too. Prufrock brought three polystyrene cups of tea and three chocolate biscuits on a tray. 'I don't suppose they've told you any more than they've told us?'

The constable shook his head. 'Wait and see; wait and see.' He picked the wrapping morosely off his biscuit.

'What about Shad's mother? Have you had any success finding her?'

Again the shake of the head. 'She was in Southend up to a month ago; then she told people she was going on holiday. No one's so much as had a postcard from her since.'

'Thank heaven for that,' said Prufrock fervently, and Fee barked a little laugh, leaving the policeman perplexed.

There was a message waiting on Rosie's desk: 'My office, soon as you get in. Dan.' Brief and to the point; like what he'd say when she got there. 'Sorry, Rosie, but this isn't what we bargained for. Too risky. Too time-consuming. I can't have you out of town for days at a time. I need you here, telling teenage girls what to do about acne and contraception. We're going to have to rethink the whole concept. Unless you'd sooner call it a day here and now . . .?'

And how would she answer? If life at the *Chronicle* would henceforth be only a diet of lovelorn bimbettes and how to get wine stains out of soft furnishings she'd just as soon park her pen. Perhaps the idea had been ill-conceived: she hadn't the patience to care about people's petty self-made problems or the skill to deal with their major ones. It might be better to quit now, gracefully, rather than wait to be sacked. It was nobody's fault: Matt hadn't the experience to know what a disaster she'd be as women's page editor and Dan, who had, had been presented with a *fait accompli*. For a time it had seemed to work, but it was mostly novelty value. At the first real test she'd so misjudged the situation that people had almost died.

She had no defence to the accusation that a competent person would have known how far to go with this and stepped back long before guns and speeding vehicles became involved. She agreed: it probably would be best if she handed over to someone who could care about the miseries of acne and two-timing boyfriends. Maybe Alex would do it. She'd do a good job, without getting the *Chronicle* into deep shit at regular intervals.

But Rosie was terribly reluctant to go. She knew she'd cocked up; she knew that, though she would try not to, she would cock up again. The pity was, she could have done some good here. She wanted another crack at it. She didn't want to pass on what she'd created to someone, even Alex, whose brief was playing safe, filling the space allotted for the least amount of risk. *The Primrose Path* had made every mistake in the book, but it had been brave and it had been honest. She didn't want to see it reduced to blandness, something for everyone and nothing to offend your maiden aunt, read it over your coffee and then do the crossword. It had been better than that. Rosie was disappointed, angry with herself, that she'd had the chance and squandered it.

'Oh, well,' she sighed, 'back down the Job Centre on Monday.' This was sheer self-indulgence: she'd never been in a job centre in her life. She went downstairs to Dan's office.

She found them together, the editor and the proprietor. They traded cautious nods. Matt had a black eye.

'Any news from the hospital?'

Rosie shook her head. 'I left Fee and Prufrock there. They'll call if there's any change.'

Dan cleared his throat. This was going to be awkward and he wanted to get it done. 'We've been getting phone calls.'

Rosie settled into a chair like a tortoise shrugging the redoubt of its shell up around it. 'I can imagine.'

'Thing is, this is an opportunist industry. Chances come along, you take them or you don't. You never know whether you were right. Big openings can lead nowhere; on the other hand, something more modest can in the long run get you where you want to be. Do you follow?'

'No,' said Rosie honestly. If he'd asked, Do you know what I'm trying to say, she'd probably have answered Yes.

The editor scowled. He knew he wasn't doing this well. In his anxiety to avoid misunderstandings he was spreading them all round like an over-enthusiastic sower. 'All right. Bottom line? Bottom line is, if you want

253

another job—'

'You won't stand in my way,' finished Rosie flatly. She couldn't even find it in her heart to be bitter.

'What? Well, no, I suppose not. But—'

'But?'

At this rate it was going to take all day. Matt stepped in. 'What you've done since coming here hasn't gone unnoticed. In the industry, I mean. The business in Edinburgh is in all the Sundays, but apart from that it was only a matter of time before you started getting offers. You're a property, Rosie. If you want to go national you could have a choice of two papers today, more by next week if you let it be known that you're interested. We'll understand if you feel your career demands that but we'd be sorry to see you go. I don't want to pressurize you but without *The Primrose Path* the *Chronicle's* future could be pretty iffy.

'So we've been trying to work out a package that'll advance your career, pay you what you're worth, give you the circulation you deserve and still keep you here. What we've come up with is a franchise: *The Path* to appear in the *Chronicle* and one of the Sundays. We can discuss the details but you'd be a lot better off, we'd get something out of it, most importantly you'd stay here instead of swanning off to London. Unless your heart's set on that.'

When she still offered no comment Matt

254

smiled wryly. 'You're in the driving seat, Rosie. You're going to have to tell us what you want. If we can reach an agreement, from our point of view the terms are secondary. If we could afford it *we'd* pay you what you're worth; since we can't we're hoping this is a way to keep you here. At least think about it,' he added anxiously, misinterpreting the amazement in her eyes, afraid she was going to refuse out of hand.

'I will.' She blinked. 'OK, I've thought. I'll stay. On two conditions.'

'Which are?' Matt made no effort to disguise his delight but Dan wanted chapter and verse.

'One, that we take a new photograph for the logo. It drives Alex crazy every week and she's right, one day it'll blow up in our faces. Maybe we could fudge it? A picture of her and me together but without a caption saying who's who? If people want to assume Primrose Holland is the good-looking one and I'm some menopausal inadequate she's advising, so be it.'

Dan nodded warily. 'And the other condition?'

She was careful about the words she used because she needed them to express accurately how she felt. 'That however successful this thing becomes, even if it *is* a significant factor in the paper's profitability, you'll remember that I'm pretty new to it. I'm not an expert. I've no training in this field and not much experience. You have cub reporters better qualified to do it than me.

'I need you to keep your hand on the reins, Dan. I'm grateful to both of you for your confidence, glad you've let me take chances that maybe cautious self-interest would have advised against. But I don't want you worrying that I'll shoot off to Docklands the first time we disagree about something. I'd back Dan's judgement against mine any day. I'm glad the page is a success, but all the more reason not to change what's worked so far, which is my hand on the steering-wheel and your foot on the brake. I need telling if I'm taking too many risks, if I'm getting out of my depth. I don't want enough rope to hang myself.'

Dan Sale, who hadn't seen a mixed metaphor like that in twenty-five years' sub-editing, harrumphed and smiled saturninely into the hands folded on his desk. 'We should go ahead with the franchise?'

That last speech had exhausted even Rosie's vocabulary. 'Yes.'

They were still grinning at one another when Dan's phone rang. He answered it, held it out. 'It's for you.'

Thinking it was the hospital Rosie took it where she sat. But it was an inquiry to *The Primrose Path*.

The young woman caller had deliberately chosen a Sunday in the hope that she could leave a message on an answering machine. She was taken aback to find herself speaking to

Primrose Holland in person. She'd have been horrified to know that her intimate concerns were being discussed in front of two men. Rosie waved them to silence.

She introduced herself as Emerald, in a Midlands accent with a faint Caribbean lilt on top. She was worrying about her forthcoming nuptials. 'He's a nice boy, a lovely boy, but he's Irish.'

'And the family don't approve.'

'No, they like him. My Mam says if he'd been ten years older she'd have had a crack at him herself. My dad says if *he'd* been ten years older he'd have encouraged her.'

'Then—?'

'He's a Catholic. Not an out-and-out God-botherer, but he takes it seriously enough that we're doing the whole church thing. And afterwards—' She came delicately to a halt.

Rosie got the picture. 'You want to put off having children, and he's not happy with contraception.'

'We're only twenty,' explained Emerald. 'We're both in work, and we need the money to set up home. But I don't want to do anything he's really uncomfortable with and I don't want to go behind his back. I wondered if there was some way of compromising, something we haven't thought of. He should be doing this,' she added with some asperity, 'he's the one with the religious scruples. But you want anything more complicated than a plug wiring

257

and you're on your own.'

'You have already come to terms with one of the fundamentals of the married state,' Rosie intoned solemnly. 'So let's tackle the other. As I understand it the Catholic Church rejects what it calls artificial methods of contraception: it has no problem with the two of you being a bit careful. There's a rather quaint expression for it: the Rhythm Method.

'Now, there's also an expression for people who follow the Rhythm Method for too long, and it's Parents. But if you're willing to take that chance, you're just wanting to defer the happy event a while, it might serve you well enough. Tell your fiancé to conquer his blushes and talk to his priest about it. And you talk to your doctor.'

'The Rhythm Method?'

'The Rhythm Method.'

Suddenly there was a deep-throated gust of laughter coming from the phone. 'You're having me on, Miss Holland! Where we going to find a steel band at three o'clock in the morning?'

*   *   *

When there was nothing more to do but think, Rosie left for home, only to find herself turning in at the hospital gates.

Fee had left half an hour before—getting that dress out, Rosie hoped. Prufrock was asleep in a chair in the waiting area. She didn't

258

disturb him, raised an interrogative eyebrow at the nurse, and getting a permissive nod in reply went through to the ward.

Changes were apparent. Much of the hardware around Shad's bed had gone. The dressing which had covered half his face had been replaced by a smaller one which showed the massive bruising in all its glory. The air-line had been removed.

At first glance the injured man still lay as quiet under the sheet as before, his visible eye shut, his bare chest rising and falling just perceptibly. But somehow there was a difference. The effect was more relaxed, less constrained. He looked bigger, as if some of the lost life-force had been pumped back into him. Sedation was yielding to sleep.

So the nurse had been right: Shad Lucas was a keeper. Rosie wondered how long before they'd know the rest: how much damage had been done, how much of it would never be put right.

As she stood by the bed she saw the metre of his breathing change, lose its perfect regularity, the movement of his chest deepen. The bruised eyelid flickered and his dry lips parted. Over the next minutes Rosie watched the animation inch back into his battered face, taking up the slackness and trying out weak but recognizable expressions of discomfort, confusion, even irritation. In the time it took him to crank the lid up to half-mast his bloodshot eye was more or less focused and he regarded her sourly.

'Hi,' said Rosie, unable to stop herself smiling.

His lips moved. She couldn't catch what he said, bent nearer. 'Say again?'

'My bloody head hurts.'

She chuckled and pulled up a chair. 'Of course it does. Have you any idea what it's been through?'

He was so long answering Rosie was beginning to think he'd gone back to sleep. Another possibility was that the neural pathways linking understanding and response were blocked. She waited, and tried not to become anxious, and by and large failed.

Finally, when she was almost ready to give up, he whispered, 'Somebody shot me.'

Relief swelled in her throat so she had to force the words out. 'Yes. Outside Prufrock's house. You remember that?'

Again the pause, not as long this time. 'He was waiting by the car. He stuck a gun in my face, and said—something—and shot me. Christ!' The terror of that struck him three days late and his body spasmed as if it had just happened.

'Gently, Shad.' Rosie laid her hand on his arm. 'It's all right, you're safe.' She frowned. 'What did he say?'

Shad shook his head, a millimetric movement on the pillow. 'He said, Hello. And then he shot me.'

'Hello?' Such politeness seemed bizarre even from a nicely brought-up assassin. 'Are you sure?' She tried it in her mouth; then she tried again with a Chinese accent. Understanding at last, she nodded and smiled. '*Gweilo.*'

'Yes. What . . .?'

'It's a Chinese insult. It means ghost—because we're white and our round eyes look like holes in a sheet to them.'

'I was shot by a Chinese?' He mulled over that for a minute. 'By a rude Chinese?'

Rosie laughed. 'You can't get much ruder than shooting somebody in the face. Shad, I will explain when you're a bit stronger. It all makes more sense than you might think. All you need to know now is, everything's fine. Fee got her brother back and neither he nor anyone else was hurt. This'—she gestured awkwardly at the bed—'was a hell of a price to pay, but we did achieve what we set out to. I don't suppose that's a lot of comfort.'

He didn't attempt to answer that just yet. Another minute passed. Then he said, 'Am I making sense?'

'Perfect sense,' said Rosie firmly.

'I could have imagined you said that.'

'You could have imagined you were shot.'

Another pause for thought. 'I didn't imagine that. That was definitely you.'

She eyed him fondly, moved her hand under his. 'You know what doctors are like, they hate to express an opinion that might be quoted back at them? Well, pathologists aren't like that. For one thing our patients don't often do anything unexpected. And I'm not your doctor, I'm your friend, and I'm as sure as I need be there is nothing wrong with your mind. Grip my hand.' He did. She moved round the bed. 'Other one.' Again, he did. She uncovered his feet. 'Make like Georgie Best.'

'Who?'

'Oh God,' she groaned, feeling her age. 'Kick, will you?' There was little enough strength there but his body was doing what he told it. 'It might be a few days before you're on your feet but you'll get there.'

'What about . . .?'

She couldn't tell whether the gaze of his bloodshot eye was hopeful or afraid, whether his extraordinary perception was something he could lose without regret or if it would be like being torn in two. She shrugged. 'You tell me.'

He searched for it but his face remained irresolute. 'I don't know. I'm not sure.'

'It may take a little time. Just because you've woken up doesn't mean it's ready to.'

'Or maybe it's gone. Destroyed.'

She saw no reason to lie. 'That, too, is possible.'

He didn't say how he felt about it. He didn't say much more at all; the lid was already drooping over his eye. Rosie knew if she turned away he'd be asleep before she reached the door. 'Get some rest. I'll see you later.'

At the door she looked back. He was still, just barely, hanging on to consciousness. He mumbled, 'My mother . . .'

'They're searching for her, Shad. She left the show to go on holiday and nobody knows where. They're leaving messages all over the place, but . . .' She didn't bother to finish the sentence. No one was listening.

Outside she told the nurse what had happened. She was going to wake Prufrock and tell him, too, but on reflection decided they might as well both sleep until at least one of them woke up naturally. She headed for the stairs.

A woman was coming up as she went down: a striking sort of woman, black hair piled high on her head, an old-fashioned hour-glass figure shown off by a suit the colour of ruby glass and heels high enough to count as an offensive weapon. A silk scarf draped through the collar of her jacket was pinned at the shoulder by a jewel so gaudy it almost had to be genuine.

Rosie blinked. It was like looking at a Rorschach test and actually seeing something in the ink-blots. 'Mrs Lucas?'

Shad's mother looked at her in surprise. 'You know me?'

'I know your son.' Rosie began to smile. The implications of Shad's last mumbled words before sleep took him were dawning on her even as they spoke. 'He said you were coming.'

263

We hope you have enjoyed this Large Print book. Other Chivers Press or Thorndike Press Large Print books are available at your library or directly from the publishers.

For more information about current and forthcoming titles, please call or write, without obligation, to:

Chivers Press Limited
Windsor Bridge Road
Bath BA2 3AX
England
Tel. (01225) 335336

OR

Thorndike Press
P.O. Box 159
Thorndike, Maine 04986
USA
Tel. (800) 223-2336

All our Large Print titles are designed for easy reading, and all our books are made to last.